LOVE FOR THE SIMONVERSE NOVELS

SIMON VS. THE HOMO SAPIENS AGENDA

William C. Morris YA Debut Award Winner

Longlisted for the National Book Award

Now a major motion picture, *Love, Simon*

"Worthy of *Fault in Our Stars*–level obsession."
—*Entertainment Weekly*

THE UPSIDE OF UNREQUITED

Seventeen Magazine Best Book

"I have such a crush on this book! Not only is this one
a must-read, but it's a must-reread."—Julie Murphy,
New York Times bestselling author of *Dumplin'*

"Heart-fluttering, honest, and hilarious.
I can't stop hugging this book."—Stephanie Perkins,
New York Times bestselling author of *Anna and the French Kiss*

★ "A fresh, honest, inclusive look at dating, families,
and friendship."—*SLJ* (starred review)

LEAH ON THE OFFBEAT

#1 *New York Times* bestseller

★ "Albertalli has a fantastic ear for voice, and it's beautifully on display
in Leah's funny, wry, and vulnerable first-person narrative."
—ALA *Booklist* (starred review)

★ "A subversive take on the coming-of-age romance
that will leave readers feeling like witnesses to a very special moment
in Leah's life and filled with gratitude for sharing it."
—*Kirkus Reviews* (starred review)

LOVE, CREEKWOOD

A SIMONVERSE NOVELLA

by Becky Albertalli

BALZER + BRAY

An Imprint of HarperCollins*Publishers*

The author is donating 100 percent of her royalty advance to The Trevor Project, the leading national organization providing crisis intervention and suicide prevention services to lesbian, gay, bisexual, transgender, queer & questioning (LGBTQ+) young people under twenty-five.

Balzer + Bray is an imprint of HarperCollins Publishers.

Library of Congress Control Number: 2020937095
ISBN 978-0-06-304813-3

Typography by Torberg Davern
21 22 23 24 25 PC/LSCH 10 9 8 7 6 5 4 3 2 1
❖
First trade paperback edition, 2021

For Creekwood's own Amy Austin,
my forever PT

Wow. Hi. This is weird, right? I swear, a part of me believes this email is going to land in your inbox circa junior year of high school. Remember when we were two oblivious dumbasses emailing from across the lunch table? As opposed to 117 and 1/2 miles away?

117. And a half. Miles away. WHO ALLOWED THIS??

So yeah, email sucks, because I want to see your face (and touch your face and smell your face and put my face on your face) (because I miss you) (I MISS YOU).

(I hate this.)

I'm not doing this right. I've forgotten how to do emails. Especially to you. How does this go again?

Dear Blue. Dear Bram. I love you. I miss you. I wish you were next to me on this shitty dorm bed with its sad little mattress, and btw I've eaten OREOS thicker than this mattress, but ANYWAY. Let's try this again, with a little positivity (yay! wheeee!).

Hi! I'm in college! And it's nice here! Everything's nice! My customs group is nice! I miss my fucking boyfriend!

1

Fuck this,

Simon aka Jacques aka your sad, pining boyfriend who is HANDLING THIS VERY POORLY

FROM: BLUEGREEN118@GMAIL.COM
TO: HOURTOHOUR.NOTETONOTE@GMAIL.COM
DATE: AUG 28 AT 11:17 PM
SUBJECT: RE: I DON'T LIKE THIS

Dear Jacques,

Sorry it took me so long to reply to your email. You can blame it on the cute college boy who FaceTimed me five minutes after he sent it.

Well, I miss you. So much. I didn't think it would hit me this quickly. It seems impossible that fifteen hours ago, I was waking up beside you in the (weirdly fancy??) Newark airport DoubleTree, and now I'm here. And you're there.

New York City feels so empty without you in it. Is that weird? You were only here for two hours. You left your mark, Simon Spier. And, no, I won't tell your mom you drove me into the city. (I love that you drove me into the city.) (Also, you're *never* allowed to drive in Manhattan ever again. I'd like to grow old with you, thank you very much.)

Anyway, nothing I write feels remotely adequate right now. I miss you. I love you. I hope you're finally settling in. Glad your roommate's such a devoted Stephen King fan, and I'm sure that giant Pennywise poster will be a joy to wake up to. Do you think you'll sleep tonight? I don't think I will. But I don't mind being a zombie for orientation, because my theory is that zombie brain will make the weeks go faster. I just need it to be September twenty-first. You know how people strike off dates on a calendar? I want a clock where I can strike off every single second.

TL; DR: I miss my fucking boyfriend too.

Love,
Blue

Okay, I have to admit, I thought you were full of shit with this one, but the link checks out. Wow, Simon, wow. There's a nerd frat at your school. That is a thing that exists. Apparently this place was made for you. And, hey, what a revelation for orientation week.

So I guess we're emailing now. Pretty adorable, Spier. Walk me through the rules here. Are we still allowed to text? Or is this just a pit stop on the way to your true boomer agenda of handwritten cards in the mail? I'm not saying I mind it. Maybe Abby and I should start doing the whole email thing too, since I'm pretty sure her new Android hates my iPhone. Seriously, don't ever fall for a girl who can't iMessage. It's the worst. Abby's the worst (she says hi!).

Also, I'm an asshole for complaining about iMessage when the *actual* worst thing is you being in Philadelphia. I miss you. And I can't even imagine what the last few days must have been like for you and Bram. You seem . . . okay? Seriously, though, vent to me anytime you want. And feel free to smack me if I start getting insufferable about Abby. I'm pretty sure I suck at this whole girlfriend thing. Forget college—they should make orientations for being in relationships. Half the time, I don't even know who I am anymore. WTF is this giddiness?

Anyway, everything's good here, just busy. I don't know why all of your weird northeastern schools start so late, but we're coming up on the first set of exams here. You know what's no joke? Timed essay tests on Elizabethan poetry. So enjoy your freedom while it lasts, Simon. Go live your wild orientation-week life doing shots of butterbeer or whatever the fuck at your nerd frat.

Did I mention I miss you?

FROM: LEAHONTHEOFFBEAT@GMAIL.COM

TO: ABBYSUSO710@GMAIL.COM

DATE: SEP 9 AT 11:51 AM

SUBJECT: WAKE UP, ABBY

I don't know how you do it, Abby Suso, but it's almost noon and you're still sleeping. Remember that drunk girl on the quad who was mad she couldn't bring a guy home to make out because her roommate was there sleeping? Abby, you are the sleeping roommate who is preventing my makeouts. Can I file a formal complaint about this?

You're so cute, though. Look at you. You're just this lump of blankets on the bed with one elbow sticking out.

Anyway, this is me sending you love letters like Simon and Bram, because they're gross, and we should be more gross. So wake up and respond to this email, okay? Doesn't have to be in writing.

Respectfully,
LCB

FROM: BLUEGREEN118@GMAIL.COM

TO: HOURTOHOUR.NOTETONOTE@GMAIL.COM

DATE: SEP 10 AT 10:10 PM

SUBJECT: RE: I DON'T LIKE THIS

Jacques,

You know what's been an unexpectedly hard adjustment? The fact that we don't know all the same people anymore. I know that's such a weird thing to miss. But it was really its own kind of language, having all those people in common: Garrett and Abby and Leah and Nick and everyone, even Martin. And now I'm surrounded by people you've never met, and you're surrounded by people I've never met, and I don't know, Simon. I really miss inhabiting your universe.

Okay, I just stopped and counted up the number of days since we've seen each other, and it's been less than two weeks. Thirteen days. I bet you haven't even done laundry yet, have you? God, I miss you. I miss you every single second.

I want to know every detail about your life, okay? I want to know about Kellan and his Stephen King fetish, and whether you're wearing shower shoes to the bathroom, and who the most annoying person is in every single one of your classes. I want the stuff you think is too boring to share.

Here's my update: I had peanut butter toast for breakfast. Best class of the day was poli-sci, because we had this amazing lecture about spotting misinformation in news articles (I'll save the real geeking out for FaceTime so you can properly make fun of me). Also, I think you may be right about that girl Ella with the tongue piercing. She caught a glimpse of my lock screen today and was weirdly flustered about it? But it actually ended up being a fun conversation. She was really curious about you ("What's his name? How soon is he transferring here? Why's he wearing a tux in an American Girl store?" ALL VERY GOOD QUESTIONS).

What else? Hmm. The libertarian edgelord from econ blessed us today with some brilliant advocacy on behalf of the devil! I know I loved being stuck in class an extra fifteen minutes to really soak in that game-changing wisdom. Then I showered and did some problem sets and fell madly in love with your latest Instagram selfie (excuse me, how is your face even legal?). And I had peanut butter toast again for dinner, because there's nothing more delicious than not walking into a giant dining hall full of strangers.

So that was my day. I didn't stop missing you for a minute. How was yours?

Love,
Blue

FROM: HOURTOHOUR.NOTETONOTE@GMAIL.COM
TO: BLUEGREEN118@GMAIL.COM
DATE: SEP 11 AT 12:07 AM
SUBJECT: RE: I DON'T LIKE THIS

"I really miss inhabiting your universe." Hello, is that a euphemism?? And in related news, can we discuss your intentions re: the phrase "unexpectedly hard"????

I miss you. Yup. Every minute. Every second. Honestly, missing you feels like the whole point of my day. Which kind of scares me, you know? Is it supposed to feel like this? Why did I think it would be easier? But Bram, hear me out. I think I left half my heart in your dorm room.

Ah yes, the libertarian edgelord. What a treat. Have I told you about the one in my psych class? Front row, gelled-up bangs, passionately defending the Stanford Prison Experiment by day three of class. Not gonna lie, I'm starting to suspect they plant one of these dudes in every 101 class as part of some big social psychology experiment. Or maybe . . . maybe COLLEGE ITSELF is one big social psych experiment, and we're the test subjects. *cue dramatic music* *close-up on my gaping-mouthed face*

Okay. My day. Let's see. Kellan was up at five thirty, *noisily* screwing in a Pennywise light switch cover. B, I'm not even convinced this is about Stephen King. I think he just really likes Pennywise. Maybe clowns in general. Anyway! I guess my day was basically like yours. Class, shower, etc. No comment re: the shower shoes. I don't really have any girls in love with me though (I TOLD YOU, BRAM. I TOLD YOU). I think people are clocking me as gay, maybe? Could it be the rainbow shoelaces? Or the fact that I'm incapable of going five minutes without mentioning my boyfriend?? Anyway, I like it. It's refreshing!

To respond to Ella's most excellent questions:

1. My name: His Royal Highness Simon Irvin Lovesick Sad Bramless Spier the first, of Oreo House.
2. DON'T TEMPT ME.
3. Garrett Laughlin.

Now go eat some real food, okay? I love you way too much to let you miss out on dining hall grilled cheese.

Sincerely,
HRH Simon ILSB Spier

FROM: ABBYSUSO710@GMAIL.COM
TO: LEAHONTHEOFFBEAT@GMAIL.COM
DATE: SEP 20 AT 12:17 AM
SUBJECT: HAPPY

Guess what—it's your birthday!!! I know it's weird to be email-ing you when you're currently sleeping two feet away from my desk, but listen up, freckle face. I have to tell you something, and I don't trust myself to say this properly when you're making bedroom eyes at me (don't deny it. You think I don't know what your bedroom eyes look like? *I live in your bedroom*).

So here's the deal: I know four-letter L words scare you (which, not gonna lie, is a BOLD stance coming from a girl whose name is literally a four-letter L word). But the truth is, I don't need you to declare a single thing, because it's written all over your face. Those are the facts. You come with subtitles, and you don't even realize it.

Hate to break it to you, Leah Burke, but you're in love with me.

I can't stop thinking about the game last Saturday. I swear, I'm grinning my face off right now. Just the thought of my nerdy drummer girlfriend earnestly typing into her phone for two hours, not even glancing up for touchdowns. Didn't think it was possible to crank out an entire sociology essay in your notes app *during a division one college football game*. But then again, it's you.

You in your Creekwood homecoming shirt with the collar cut wide. Me, openly spellbound by your shoulder freckles. So many mysteries all wrapped up in one girl. Like the fact that Leah "fuck homecoming" Burke somehow managed to acquire a CHS homecoming shirt in the first place. Or the fact that you wore it to a UGA home game. I don't know if you noticed the *tens of thousands of people* in the stands wearing red. But I loved how little it fazed you, no self-consciousness whatsoever (this from a girl who double-proofreads every Instagram caption). You, Leah Burke, are an encyclopedia of contradictions.

(Like how you won't admit you're in love with me! And yet you'll email me love letters!)

Well, birthday girl, how's this for a love letter: I'm head over heels for you, Leah. And if you ever want to try out one of those scary four-letter L words on me, I promise I'll say it back.

xoxo,

Abby

FROM: SIMONIRVINSPIER@GMAIL.COM

TO: LEAHONTHEOFFBEAT@GMAIL.COM

DATE: SEP 20 AT 3:13 PM

SUBJECT: YOU WERE BORN!!!

HEY, LEAH, IT'S YOUR BIRTHDAY!!!!!! So here's your birthday email, not to be confused with your birthday texts or the voicemail I left you at 9:20 a.m. or the one I'm definitely going to leave you at 9:20 p.m. (phone alarm is locked and loaded). Well, I hope you're out on the town right now, living that charmed nineteen-year-old midafternoon life. God, it's so weird not seeing you on your birthday. I want to hear about everything. How are your classes—how's sociology? How's everything with Abby? Did you talk to Nick? He said he was going to call you early, because Taylor wants to go to the symphony orchestra in Boston, which she apparently thinks is a Shawn Mendes concert or something, because she's insisting they get there two hours early "just in case." And Nick's just like, "oh well, gotta keep the girlfriend happy." Leah, my jaw dropped. GIRLFRIEND?? Did you know about this development? Because I sure the fuck didn't. Our Nick, sealing the deal with Taylor freaking Metternich. What a JOURNEY.

Aaaaaand speaking of shitshows (sorry, I realize this email

is like 90 percent gossip, but I keep forgetting to text you this golden information), have you heard anything about Garrett and Morgan? I can't 100 percent confirm this one, since it's coming secondhand from Nick, but apparently Morgan was up at Tech last weekend? Morgan Hirsch at Georgia Tech??? There can only be one explanation for this, and it starts with M and rhymes with takeout. Of course, Garrett's currently denying everything, but Bram's working on getting more info, so stay tuned!

Anyway, I miss your face and your voice and god I wish you were here with me at Haverford, doodling in the margins of all my notes. And I hope you're having the best birthday ever. I love you so much, beautiful Leah, and I'm so glad you were born.

Love,
Simon

Dear Jacques,

I hate everything. I hate every white square on my calendar. I doubt you're even past Newark, but you might as well be halfway to Mars, because either way, I can't kiss you again for another twelve days.

Can we just rewind to Friday afternoon? I keep scrolling back to your text saying you were *finally* pulling into Penn Station (look, I'm not trying to be dramatic about this, but it was starting to feel like your train was being pulled by a single elderly mule). But then you stepped into the concourse in your Haverford sweatpants, looking so bowled over by the entire concept of Manhattan.

Simon, I don't know if you noticed the *giant Oreo donut sign* outside Krispy Kreme, but you ran straight past it, into my arms (greatest compliment of my life, hands down). And then I held your face and kissed you in the middle of Penn Station, because apparently public kissing is a thing I do now. What's your deal, Simon Spier? Are you made of magnets or what?

Anyway, now I'm sitting here staring at my laptop, trying to find the words to explain how it felt to have you here again. I . . . don't even have a frame of reference for it. Like, I keep thinking about Garrett, and how it's been a month since I've seen him. And that sucks, don't get me wrong, but it's like going a month without waffles or something. Not seeing you until your fall break? That's like twelve days without water.

And now I miss you even more, because you're all over my dorm room. The Oreo boxes in my trash can, the song lyrics on my whiteboard. Even this laptop. How am I ever going to use it for homework when it just makes me miss watching your absolute shitshow top thirty life hack videos on YouTube? (For the record, though, I do NOT miss those shitshow videos. I just miss you leaning your head on my shoulder while we *watched* those shitshow videos.)

And then there's my bed. How am I ever going to sleep there again without remembering how little sleeping we did in it?

Love,
Blue

Abraham. Romeo. Greenfeld. I think I need a minute here. (Not for that. Mind out of the gutter. I just have to, like, catch my breath. Or something.) I mean, THAT? That was a love letter. Bram, I'm *blushing*. This is junior year all over again. I feel like my secret email boyfriend just told me he imagines me fantasizing about sex (HEY BLUE, REMEMBER THAT?).

I swear, everyone thinks you're so freaking innocent, but then you sign into gmail and it's like BAM. Innuendo. Sex grenade. *How little sleeping we did??* I mean, you're not wrong, but WOW. And the best part's how you had this whole food itinerary, with the Dinosaur Bar-B-Que restaurant and the hipster ice cream parlor. Which I'm sure are delicious (who doesn't love eating dinosaurs?). But peanut butter toast and never leaving your dorm room tasted pretty great, too. ☺

A FEW IMPORTANT CORRECTIONS. First things first: "I always wanted to stumble into someone like you." That, sir, is no song lyric. It's a book quote (does this mean there's a book on this earth you haven't read yet??). Second things second, shitshow?? Are you saying you *don't* need a succulent vase made out of a spray-painted doll's head?

God, I'm so bad at this. Here I am going on about dinosaurs

and YouTube and 5-Minute Crafts, when all I really want is to write is I miss you. Because HOLY SHIT, I MISS YOU. You know, I thought I was fine when I boarded the train. But then you texted me our selfie from Shake Shack, and that was it. That picture. It was just so *us*, with me looking like I was going to burst out laughing, and you with that deer-in-the-headlights, anime-eyes face you get whenever there's a straw in your mouth. Bram, it destroyed me. Like, it just hit me all of a sudden how that moment is OVER. And we'll never, ever get it back. (God, even as I'm writing this, I know it's so weird and over-the-top. Look at me having an existential crisis over a five-minute pit stop at Shake Shack.)

But I kept thinking about last year, and the year before that, and how being near you was this everyday thing I took completely for granted. And we don't get to go back. We don't get to do high school again. And, yeah, I knew that intellectually, but I don't think I fully processed it until now. I guess being on a literal express train away from you really made it sink in.

So now I'm back in my room with Kellan and his friend Grover (no REALLY), who has a guitar, and can sing, and is currently playing "Hey There Delilah" for the twentieth time. I think he's trying to teach it to himself. I feel like I should be annoyed, but I'm just so drained. And now that song's stuck in my head, and Bram, I don't know if you know the lyrics to that one, but it's like . . . too freaking relevant. So now I feel like crying again, but I don't want to do that in front of a bunch of random straight dudes. Maybe I'm not cut out for this whole roommate thing. Like, I want to know who thought it was a good idea to stick a random guy in my room and have him *live* there.

But mark my words, Greenfeld: We're going to be Kellan-free for fall break. I will make it my life's fucking mission.

Twelve more days. God, I miss you. And I love you. I'm, like, preposterously in love with you.

Love,
Simon

FROM: ABBYSUSO710@GMAIL.COM
TO: SIMONIRVINSPIER@GMAIL.COM
DATE: SEP 30 AT 11:21 PM
SUBJECT: RE: A QUESTION

I've got to say, that's the weirdest fucking question you've ever asked me (AND I LOVE IT). So let's make sure I'm following this. You want your roommate to leave early for fall break. And for that to happen, you need me (me!) to come up with a list of, and I quote, "clown-centered DC attractions"? WELL THEN.

First of all, Simon, are we sure *clown-centered* is a thing? Because it looks like we just found a hot new contender for Most Cursed Adjective (you had a good run, *moist*). Seriously, though, what does that even mean? Clown-centered? Is that a metaphor? Are we talking about GOP senators, or do you mean literal, actual clowns? And if so, WTF?? Do you just really hate your roommate? I have SO MANY QUESTIONS.

But yeah! Happy to see if Molly and Cassie have heard of anything . . . clown-centered. They're at University of Maryland now, though, which is outside the city. Is that okay, or do you need it to be in DC proper? (Seriously, I am DYING to know what your roommate did to deserve this.) Anyway, texting M and C in a sec, and I'll report back!

So, other than scheming against your roommate, what on earth are you up to? And how was New York? Leah and I actually heard from Nick this morning, by the way. Can you believe it?? He wanted to know if we're coming home this weekend (we are, for what it's worth, in case you were maaaaaybe considering coming down early?).

Anyway, Nick said he talked to Bram, and he got the impression that you two are kind of struggling with the long-distance stuff, I guess? I don't want to overstep or anything, but I did want to make sure you're okay. You always seem so cheerful with me, and that's great, seriously. But I hope you know I'm here if you ever want to talk through the hard stuff. And same with Leah. We both love you so much, Si.

(And in happier Bram news, tell him congrats from me on the game!!)

Anyway, write back soon so I can start sorting through all your clown shit!! MISS YOU!!!

xoxo
Abby

Clown-centered attractions are totally a thing!! I'm thinking circuses, funhouses, clown museums (I feel like clown museums exist, probably?). Anyway, GREAT question, but nope, not a metaphor. And DC suburbs are fine—I think Kellan's parents actually live in the suburbs, now that you mention it. And by the way, I don't hate Kellan!! But he says he's hanging around campus the first part of fall break, and I need him to GTFO and go home early to be with his clowns. He *likes* clowns. A lot. (Anyway, tell Molly and Cassie thank you from me!)

So, Bram and me.

First of all, Abby, you're not overstepping! I'm sorry I haven't been more open about stuff. I just feel so weird about the whole thing. I guess I didn't expect it to be this hard. Which is probably really naive of me? But the thing is, so many couples do this! All the time! And in the grand scheme of things, New York to Philly is *nothing*. Like, we're so fucking lucky. I got him a week ago, and I get him back on Friday, and Abby, I don't know why this is so unbearable. I just miss him so much.

Anyway, I love you, and thank you, and hug Leah for me, okay? I mean you're probably already hugging RIGHT THIS SECOND, aren't you (is "hugging" a euphemism? I don't know, you tell me!).

Miss you too, Abby Suso. ♥

Love,
Simon

It's *so* weird. I keep looking up from my phone expecting you to be there, and nope—it's just fifty-fucking-million printed manga drawings. You're too far away. I don't like it. And I miss you, which I realize makes me downright insufferable. Oh no, I have to sleep in a different room than my girlfriend for three nights. Better cue up the world's tiniest violin.

But I'm sorry it's taken me so long to properly write back. *Someone* wanted to watch *Mamma Mia!* again (actually, make that two someones, because apparently Wells knows all the words to Dancing Queen. Who knew?). And you're on my shit list, Abby Suso, because I *never* cry at this movie. Why is *Mamma Mia!* hitting so different?? What have you done to me???

Anyway, tomorrow should be quite the fucking scene. You sure you don't want us to bring a side dish at least? I think my mom's really worried your parents will hate her. Like, she keeps talking about how excited she is, but she gets this kind of frantic look when she says it. Just to warn you, she has very little filter when she's nervous, but I'll be ready and primed to run interference if necessary. And of course, she and Wells have both gotten the full rundown of what your parents do and don't know. (I have to say, I kind of love the fact that your parents know I'm your girlfriend. They just don't know I'm your *room-mate*. And we'll make sure they continue to not know.)

So, I'll see you soon. And until then, I'll just lie here in my childhood bed, giving over my entire existence to a certain four-letter L word. (Lazy. The word is *lazy*.) (Among others.)

Miss you, Suso.

Cordially,
LCB

FROM: ABBYSUSO710@GMAIL.COM
TO: LEAHONTHEOFFBEAT@GMAIL.COM
DATE: OCT 7 AT 9:34 PM
SUBJECT: RE: THIS IS WEIRD, RIGHT??

Happy last night without me!!!!!!! Honestly, you should be taking advantage of this. Sow all your non-Abby wild oats and . . . watch a movie with subtitles? Read a bunch of books with bookmarks? Frankly, I don't even know what you'd do without me. So maybe we scratch the whole wild oats idea and just text each other all night?

Dinner went well, don't you think? I'm pretty sure my mom wants to adopt your mom (also, I think she thinks your mom's, like, twenty-five, which is some interesting math!). Really sorry about the church thing, Leah. I promise she's not trying to make some kind of statement. She's not even that religious. She just wants to show you off to her church friends (it's actually pretty cute—she's already told them all about us, and I think she even cropped Garrett out of some of our prom pictures. Whoops!).

Definitely a close call, though, when my dad asked about your roommate. Man, you and your mom are such hilarious opposites. She's sitting there, eyes popping out of their sockets, looking like she just swallowed twenty hot peppers. But you? You just did your little half shrug and said, "She's nice. We're actually working on an anatomy project together." You didn't even glance at me for a second when you said it. You're such a goddamn flirt, Leah Burke. YOU DON'T EVEN TAKE ANATOMY. (Also you had me feeling things I should NOT be feeling at my parents' dinner table, so thanks a fuckton for that, you jerk.)

Text me when you're up. ♥

xoxo,
Abby

FROM: BLUEGREEN118@GMAIL.COM

TO: HOURTOHOUR.NOTETONOTE@GMAIL.COM

DATE: OCT 7 AT 10:11 PM

SUBJECT: RE: PRETTY SURE I MISS YOU MORE

Dear Jacques,

Well, I'm home. And I've been staring at this email for about twenty minutes, grasping around for something upbeat to say. But I'm coming up empty. It's just getting harder and harder. I can't believe I woke up this morning with your head in the crook of my neck, your hand on my chest. Simon, I can't even tell you how empty my room feels. I want to be back in Philly, looking at all the trees by the duck pond, and kissing you behind Drinker House, because apparently it really does exist (and for the record, if kissing you is my punishment, I'll happily lose every bet we ever make).

Anyway, I know you're attempting to go to bed early (and probably failing miserably. I don't know how anyone sleeps before a six a.m. flight). Did Kellan leave yet? I'm actually really glad I got to meet him. I like him! He's definitely an odd duck, but it's endearing. I mean, he clearly believes in ghosts, and I don't really get the clown thing. But he's living his truth, and I

27

have to respect that. Also, it was really cool of him to crash in Grover's room all weekend. ☺

So, is it weird knowing you'll be home tomorrow? I'm sure your parents are going to buy out the entire Oreo display at Publix. It's pretty wild that they managed to hide the whole thing from Nora. Who knew your dad had it in him? Can't wait to hear how she reacts when she sees you—and tell her happy birthday from me, okay? I really hate that I'm not coming with you. I still can't believe you have a full week off, and I'm just stuck here (with two essays due on Friday, no less). But apparently I'm doing an escape room with Ella and her friend Miriam on Saturday (she swears it's fun, and she thinks I'll be good at it? I guess we'll find out!). And then I've got a game on Sunday.

Simon, I'm so sorry I didn't tell you about soccer. And I'm sorry I had such a hard time explaining in person. I don't even have a good explanation. I guess I was weirdly embarrassed about it being an intramural league and not the school team. Which is ridiculous, I realize, for so many reasons, beginning with the fact that you're the literal last person who'd judge me for that (Simon, I'm not even sure you know what intramural sports *are*). But I felt so self-conscious about it anyway, like maybe I'm not really the soccer kid you fell in love with. And then there were the logistical factors, like how a lot of the games are on Sundays. I didn't want you to feel like we had to plan our trips around my games (my team knows I'll have to miss a few, and everyone's cool with it, I promise).

And, Simon, I think the part that feels shittiest is the fact that I'm actually really, really liking it. Which makes me feel like a terrible boyfriend. I don't know if that even makes sense. I guess it just feels like if I'm happy here, I'm basically throwing up a giant middle finger at our relationship. I know that's completely illogical, and I PROMISE it has nothing to do with anything you've ever said or done. It's just my brain being glitchy, like it always is. I don't think I've told you about that first year after we moved, but it was the same kind of thing. I was in this brand new school, in this brand new town, and every decent moment felt like a betrayal of my old life.

I just don't want you to think I miss you any less, okay? Soccer's a nice distraction, but you're the love of my life.

Love,
Blue

FROM: HOURTOHOUR.NOTETONOTE@GMAIL.COM
TO: BLUEGREEN118@GMAIL.COM
DATE: OCT 8 AT 12:10 PM
SUBJECT: THE SOCCER KID I FELL IN LOVE WITH

So, I've been thinking about your email all morning. God. I don't even know what to say. I'm just gutted, Bram. I'm so fucking sorry. The fact that you found something good, and I made you feel like you couldn't tell me. I'm the worst boyfriend on earth. But let me be totally clear: I want you to be happy. And if that's in New York or New Zealand or Antarctica or Jupiter, so be it. Bram, I love that you're playing soccer. I love that you're loving it. I love that you're happy. I love you, okay? And that's it. That's the whole entire point.

So tell me everything. I want to know about your teammates, and whether you get to wear those cute little knee socks, and if you'll get a trophy with an upside-down gold guy kicking a soccer ball. I want to know if it feels different than it did at Creekwood. Oh, and for the record, I DO know what intramurals are, thank you very much. Did you know I played intramural basketball for six months in middle school? WE EVEN WON A GAME (okay, technically the other team had to forfeit, but it was STILL A WIN).

And in other news, I'm home! Though getting here was a bit of a shitshow. I don't know why I picked a flight that landed in the middle of Atlanta morning rush hour (okay, I do know why, it was cheap, but GOD. What a mess). Also, my dad took the morning off work to pick me up, and we were going to stop at the Varsity for frosted oranges. But then the Varsity wasn't even open yet, because apparently Simon and Jack Spier are the only two dumbasses who want milkshakes at ass o'clock in the morning. But Nora's still at school, of course. Maybe I'll hide in her room with Bieber and spring up from the bed or something when she walks in there. Is that creepy, genius, or both?

Anyway, soccer kid, go be happy this week. Kick a ball around, hang with Ella, take the subway down to Brooklyn. Fall in love with New York. (And, for the love of god, go to the dining hall! You're an athlete, go eat some real food!)

I love you more than anything, okay?

Love,
Simon

FROM: SIMONIRVINSPIER@GMAIL.COM

TO: LEAHONTHEOFFBEAT@GMAIL.COM

DATE: OCT 14 AT 4:55 PM

SUBJECT: BACK IN PHILLY!!

Hey! Just letting you know I made it (and sorry for all the frantic texts). Holy shit, that was way too close for comfort. I'm surprised they even let me board. I totally had to do the walk of plane shame, where everyone's just blatantly hoping I won't take the extra seat they apparently now feel is their birthright. But I'm here, and it's weirdly nice to be back in my room again. It's even good to see Kellan. He's funny, he just asked me how my trip to Shady Creek was, like it's a normal city people have heard of. Kind of sweet that he remembered that, I guess?

It was just so, so great to see you guys—wish I could have stayed the whole weekend. I've never really just wandered around Athens before, and I'm pretty jealous of you now, because it's the coolest fucking city on earth. Like that record shop, with all the album art on the wall and all the vintage R.E.M. posters. Leah, I could lock myself inside that store and be happy for the rest of my life.

And thanks for letting me spiral about the Bram thing. I

know it's going to be fine. It's already fine. I just feel bad I made him feel like he has to hate New York to prove he misses me. And I don't want him to be sad just because I'm sad.

I mean, I don't hate it here. It's just that everything feels so muted without him. It's so hard to explain it. It's like, I'm happy sometimes, but there's a ceiling. Without Bram, I'm never more than 75 percent okay. And, Leah, I'm so scared I'm not up for four years of this. Maybe I made the wrong choice. I do love this school. It's the most beautiful place I've ever seen in real life. And I like my customs group. But I also don't really feel close to any of them. And it doesn't take a genius to figure out why. I'm not fully present. I've got one foot in New York.

Sorry, I know that's a lot. You don't have to reply to any of that. I'm just being a mopehead (my new favorite Nora-ism—can you believe our girl was today years old when she learned that the word's actually "moped"? I worry about Georgia public schools, I really do). Anyway, good luck with sociology. You're going to ace the freaking fuck out of it, of course, because you're you, and because you're adorably obsessed with that class.

Miss you, Leah.

Love,
Simon

Right, so what's actually adorable is the thought of you sitting on your little dorm bed typing the words "freaking fuck." I don't want to turn your world upside down, Spier, but the whole point of freaking is to avoid saying fuck. Freaking fuck is like ordering a Diet Coke and twenty donuts. Just say fuck, you know? Own it. Live your truth. (I did, by the way, ace the fucking fuck out of that quiz.)

Simon, listen to me: I am always, always up for a spiral. Don't apologize. This is a massive change for you guys, and I can't begin to imagine what that must feel like. Obviously, my situation right now is the opposite of long-distance, but I've definitely thought about the whole being-fully-present thing. My mom always used to talk about how she never really had an Immersive College Experience (aka Baby Me was a cockblock). Anyway, she always said she liked the idea of me starting with a total blank slate—no babies, no relationships. Don't get me wrong, she's totally all-in on Abby. But I guess I must have internalized the whole idea of it at some point, because every so often, I find myself asking what parties I'm saying no to because I'd rather stay in with my girlfriend. (And then

I remember I'm *perfectly* fucking fine saying no to parties, girlfriend or no girlfriend.)

So what I'm trying to say is I get where you're coming from, at least about the one-foot-in, one-foot-out feeling. But maybe that's just what happens when you find a person you like better than the rest of the world. You say yes to your person and no to the world, over and over and over (until you're old and married, I guess? Jesus Christ, I don't know).

Anyway, I'm so sorry you're having such a shitty time with all of this. I really hate how much you're hurting. But, Simon, you don't owe anyone your happiness. You know that, right? You can mope around and miss your boyfriend and be sad when he does stuff without you, and that's a pretty fucking normal way to feel, actually. I'm not saying you should be an asshole to him about it. But don't be an asshole to yourself either.

I love you, mopehead. Glad you made your flight.

Ms. Burke, I've taken all your concerns under advisement, and I have reached the conclusion that I'm on the right side of this issue. I intend to make my final case below. I ask only that you read it with an open mind and heart.

Reasons Why Leah Burke and Abby Suso Need to Be CatDog for Halloween: A Point-by-Point Analysis

CatDog is an underappreciated icon, who deserves all the honor and respect in the world after being overlooked for decades (by everyone but my brother, Isaac William Suso, who once had to be talked out of getting a six-inch CatDog tattoo around his bicep. But tattoos, as you can imagine, are a completely different conversation. Might I remind you that Halloween costumes are fleeting and impermanent, much like our very existence?).

CatDog, being both a cat and a dog, is therefore at least twice as creative as any single cat or dog costume.

Built-in conversation starter: CatDog's bodily functions.

CatDog can be accomplished with the barest shortlist of items (two extra-long yellow T-shirts, yellow tights, felt, glue, poster board, markers, extra fabric, face paint) (okay, it's not the *barest* shortlist, but it's cheaper than a Hogwarts robe).

Literally what could be sexier than a conjoined cat and dog??

Frankly, I kind of dig the idea of being physically attached to you all night.

In conclusion: Will you take my dog body to fuse with your cat body for as long as we both shall attend Caitlin's Halloween party this weekend?

xoxo
Abby

FROM: LEAHONTHEOFFBEAT@GMAIL.COM
TO: ABBYSUSO710@GMAIL.COM
DATE: OCT 24 AT 3:15 PM
SUBJECT: RE: HEAR ME OUT

You know, for all the hours I spent daydreaming about what it would be like to date you, I somehow failed to anticipate the involvement of CatDog. You realize CatDog is essentially a penis with animal heads on either end, right? And are the cat and dog romantically involved with each other? Are they siblings? I don't know, Suso. If we're going to walk around dressed like them all night, I feel like we should know their deal.

(I can't believe I'm letting you talk me into this. Like, I actually, seriously can't believe it, even as I'm typing this. These four-letter-L-word feelings are starting to be a PROBLEM.)

So, I'm the cat, huh?

Kind regards,
LCB

FROM: HOURTOHOUR.NOTETONOTE@GMAIL.COM

TO: BLUEGREEN118@GMAIL.COM

DATE: OCT 28 AT 3:04 AM

SUBJECT: THIS NIGHT

All right, first of all, Bramster, your latest Instagram post is a personal attack. You in a Ravenclaw robe????? Text me a warning next time or something. You know PERFECTLY WELL I now have to drop a thirsty heart-eye emoji in your comments section (where my sisters can see it!!! THANKS A LOT). You're just so fucking gorgeous. Sometimes I see a picture of you, and I'm like, *holy shit, that's my boyfriend*. I should really make a PowerPoint with pictures of you and call it Sorry, Gents, He's Taken. It'll be great, I'll make the whole world die of jealousy.

Anyway, hope you and Garrett are having a happy Halloween weekend (which should *definitely* be called Halloweekend, why aren't we doing that??) (wait, I just googled it and apparently people ARE doing it, so congrats I guess to all you Einsteins out there who made it a hashtag. Way to be a million times smarter than me). Okay, I already forgot what I'm talking about. GOD I HAVE SO MUCH TO TELL YOU, but I don't know where to start, because I'm a liiiiiittle drunk right now. Not like cartwheels-on-Founders-Green-wearing-only-Mickey-ears-level drunk (Nude Mickey, whoever you are, you were joyful and free, and I love that for you).

So guess what?? College is amaaaaazing. And before I forget, Kellan told me to tell you to go to Big Nick's Pizza, because it has the best pizza and milkshakes, and this is according to his cousin Dannon Maya who (despite being named after yogurt apparently??) is a REAL New Yorker. Wait haha sorry, it's TWO cousins, Dan AND Maya, which makes so much more sense. Needless to say, Kellan is slightly drunk and also dressed like a ventriloquist dummy (which is a plot twist I did NOT see coming . . . Kellan likes clowns *and* dummies!).

But I have to tell you about tonight, Bram, and I actually kind of want to cry right now, because I'm so relieved my brain remembers how to be happy. Tonight just felt like COLLEGE. It was exactly how I'd always pictured it. I wasn't even planning to go out, because all I had was a striped-shirt bank robber costume, aka the most basic bitch costume ever invented. But then Liza came over (can't remember if I told you about her, but she's our customs person. Kind of like an RA, I guess? Basically, she's a sophomore who lives on my hall, and she's like a big sister to our whole customs group). So Liza took me under her wing (literal wing, she was dressed like an angel) (also, she's an ACTUAL angel!). I don't even know how it happened, B, but I pulled Liza's tutu on over my jeans and polo shirt, and now I'm Billy Elliot??? ("Stranger Things Ballerina Edition" was a really good guess though, props to Garrett from me!)

So a bunch of us from my customs group ended up in this guy Jacob's room (did I mention there are two Jacobs on my hall, plus an Isaac and a Rachel? I feel like I'm living in the Old Testament. IF ONLY WE HAD AN ABRAHAM). Anyway, it was me, both Jacobs, Liza, Kellan, Grover, and this girl Jocelyn from downstairs, and I've hung out with Liza and the Jacobs before (watching TV or chatting in the bathroom, that kind of thing), but I hadn't really sat down and talked to them. So we kind of piled onto Jacob's bed, just ranting about politics and talking about all our people from home (of course they got an EARFUL about you). And then somehow there was vodka and orange juice, and we were planning to go to the big Halloween party at Bryn Mawr, but we ended up just skipping that and going to the one at Founders Hall (which is when I left you the voicemail).

I don't know, it all just felt so fun and carefree. I danced with the girls for a bit, and I had this weirdly intense conversation about pandas with someone dressed like a panda (I don't even know their name, we were in line for the bathroom). And then we were walking home, and Bram GUESS WHAT: Kellan and Grover were holding hands!!! And it turns out they've been together since orientation week, and I missed the memo because I'm just that fucking oblivious. Bram, this whole time, I really thought they were straight-bro BFFs. I'm literally that woman Marjorie from the train station ("I just have to say, it's so refreshing when young men are willing to be affectionate with their friends!"). I should just turn in my gay card. I don't even deserve to drink iced coffee at this point.

Oh god, this email is like a whole ass novel. I'm sorry!!! I just miss you so much, honey. Babe. Sweetie. Oh my god, I legit can't pull ANY of these off with a straight face. Are we just never going to have pet names? Darling??? I kind of love that one. It gives me Monty and Percy vibes (though truly, what does Percy see in that hot mess of a boy?). So, darling, I hope you and Garrett are having a most excellent Halloweekend. More pictures, please!!! I love you so much, Brammy Bram. Come back to Philly ASAP, okay, so we can show Marjorie something REALLY refreshing.

Love,
Simon, Ballerina Edition

FROM: BLUEGREEN118@GMAIL.COM
TO: HOURTOHOUR.NOTETONOTE@GMAIL.COM
DATE: OCT 29 AT 11:29 AM
SUBJECT: RE: THIS NIGHT

Dear Jacques,

Hi, darling. ☺ I very much hope you're still sleeping. So I can't decide if your email completely charmed me or completely wrecked me. Maybe both. The problem, Simon, is that drunk you sounds just like sleepy you, and thinking about sleepy Simon Spier is kind of a gut punch right now. Have I mentioned how much I miss your head on my pillow? I miss it the *most*. Especially the part where you keep nodding off while talking (which is, by the way, the *exact* energy of your email). Anyway, the point is, I'm hopelessly in love with my drunk mess of a boyfriend.

(For what it's worth, I think I know what Percy Newton sees in Henry Montague.)

Thank you very much for the thirsty emoji (both of your sisters did indeed "heart" it, as did your mom, of course). Last night was . . . fine? Don't get me wrong, it was a good haunted house. It just might have been a little *too* good (confession: I don't really see the point of haunted houses if I can't leave halfway through and make out with you in the back of Nick's car). Garrett loved it, though. He's still passed out, but I'm waking him up in a minute, since he has to get to LaGuardia by three. It was actually really awesome having him here. He caught me up on everything happening at Tech (except Morgan, because he's still insisting nothing happened. Still!). Overall, he seems happy. It does sound like he might be having trouble keeping up with the workload (I'm not sure running away to New York for the weekend was the solution to that particular problem, but I'm trying to quiet my inner nerd and let our angel bro live).

Oh, I'm so glad you finally got to have your College Feeling. I'm actually a little choked up over the thought of you in a tutu (wouldn't your kid self be proud?). It just made me really happy, in the same way your rainbow shoelaces make me happy. I love watching you try on this part of yourself. You don't have to give up a single day of iced coffee, Simon, I promise.

Tell Kellan I say thank you for the recommendation! I can save it for when you're here in December, if you want. I'm really glad to hear about him and Grover! I kind of suspected it when Kellan stayed in Grover's room that whole weekend (also, you realize Kellan has a framed picture of Harvey Milk on his desk, right?). So maybe you have a touch of Marjorie in you, but don't we all? I'm not exactly batting a thousand on this stuff either (see also: prom night).

Anyway, I love you. And I miss every edition of you. Text me when you're up, okay?

Love,
Blue

This just in: I, Abby Suso, have officially figured out the solution to *boredom itself.* Right now, I'm in Analytic Geometry and Calculus (it's just as enthralling as it sounds), but the point is: I'm emailing you!! From Analytic Geometry and Calculus!! So, here's the trick:

    Open up a Word doc.

    Title it "Anal GC" (god, I love abbreviations).

    Minimize it into a horizontal bar with the title showing, loud and proud.

    Open up a "compose email" window and slide that lil dude right under your Word doc.

    And . . . voilà! MOVE OVER, ANAL CALCULUS. Welcome to Emailing Love Letters to My Girlfriend 101, where class is *always* in session. Let's see, what's on the syllabus for this morning? Shall we discuss the geometric properties of our dorm room? Leah, much in the spirit of CatDog, I'd like to note the vast and complex advantages to be derived from merging two separate entities into one (wow, I sound like a lawyer prowling for sex). Okay, what I'm trying to say is we're *long* overdue for some strategic furniture rearrangement.

To be clear: I, Abby Nicole Suso, am officially proposing we push our beds together, and I will make my case below.

Picture this: We push my bed to your side of the room, instantly freeing up almost a *full wall* on my side (and then we cover it with those temporary, fake white brick panels for the ultimate Pottery Barn aesthetic!!!).

I am aware, of course, that having a single bed is a Statement. That said, us being literally incapable of being near each other without some form of physical contact is also a Statement. So maybe we just lean into the Statement?

WE END UP IN ONE BED 90 PERCENT OF THE TIME ANYWAY, LEAH BURKE, AND YOU KNOW IT.

I'm just saying, the analytic geometry of the situation looks pretty clear to me! (Speaking of geometry, my professor just caught my eye and gave me a satisfied nod—she is LOVING my diligent note-taking!!)

So I forgot to tell you, I talked to Simon yesterday when you were at the library! He's doing better, I think? I'm sure he told you about his cute weirdo roommate coming out (actually, I don't think Kellan was ever *not* out, but Simon is Simon is Simon). Anyway, our boy is clearly loving having a platonic gay guy BFF, and he would like us to know that Kellan has a healthy general interest in horror and paranormal phenomena, and is not, in fact, "into clowns." And apparently Kellan and his boyfriend talked him into going on some Philadelphia ghost tour on his birthday weekend?? (Um, I'm not the only one who remembers him and Bram at Netherworld last year, right?)

Anyway, it's nice to hear he's finally hanging out more with Haverford people (oh, and I finally asked about the "customs group" thing—apparently it's basically just his hallmates?). I don't know, Leah, I've been so worried about him since fall break. Didn't he just seem a little bit off when we saw him? I know the long-distance thing is hitting him really hard, and I think this is their longest stretch this semester without seeing each other. I wish I knew how Bram's holding up. Did Garrett say anything when you talked to him? Can we just, like . . . text Bram and check in? Would that be weird?

God, I don't even know how they do it. I can barely handle your bed being across the room.

Okay, class is ending in a second, so I'm rereading this really quickly before I send it, and hmmmmm I feel like it's missing some critical love letter elements. Maybe more four-letter L words would help? Just a thought!!

xoxo,
Abby

Okay, Suso, I'm trying out your methods in Intro to English Lit (but if you think I'm not still titling my doc "Anal GC," you don't even know me). Anyway, so far, so good! Question, though: Are we trying to learn any of the actual course material here, or nah?

Well, Abigail, I've reviewed your proposal, and I have no objections (other than the fact that I'm clearly setting an unfortunate precedent of being easily persuaded by multipoint lists). (God, you're going to ask me to marry you one day with a numbered fucking email list, aren't you?) But even I have to admit that points two and three are very persuasive. Pottery Barn, though. You know you're emailing me, right? Leah Burke? Not, like, Simon's mom?

Moving on to your most important question: Are you the only one who remembers Simon and Bram at Netherworld? You mean the time they both got so scared they had to be escorted, crying, out the emergency exit? I bet Simon's going to be a real treat on that ghost tour!

So, I knew about Kellan being gay. I'm thrilled to hear he's not "into clowns." (God, I'd fucking love to know how that conversation went down.) I'm really happy for Simon. And jealous, of course, because I'm a territorial asshole. But I know he deserves a gay guy best friend, too, especially one who isn't a train ride away. I do worry about him. He's been kind of a mess since August, hasn't he? Garrett says Bram's okay—he's just kind of distracted and glued to his phone a lot. I'm sure it's fine if we text him. The whole thing's just a bummer. I sort of wonder if one of them should just transfer or something. Though, Simon definitely seems more upbeat this week, so maybe I'm just being dramatic. But yeah—I don't know how they do it either. I'd have a very hard time being that far away from you.

God, I keep going back to what you said about us and physical contact. Not going to lie, Suso, that hit me like a brick to the face. You're not wrong. I just didn't really think about it until you said it. I guess it's automatic at this point. I see your hand, and I have to hold it. Your mouth exists, so I have to kiss it.

You know you terrify me, right?

Sincerely,
LCB

FROM: BLUEGREEN118@GMAIL.COM

TO: HOURTOHOUR.NOTETONOTE@GMAIL.COM

DATE: NOV 16 AT 10:02 AM

SUBJECT: THE EDGE OF NINETEEN

Dear Jacques,

Well, it's the last day of your first year of adulthood (soon to be the first day of the last year of your teens—is your head spinning yet?). I can't believe how long I've known you. I can't believe how recently I met you. My brain keeps scrolling back through all our Novembers, and I don't know how you do it, Simon, but you make memories feel like time travel. Everything uploads in high-definition when it comes to you.

Remember last year? Homecoming, when we didn't dance. And Nick's cabin afterward, when we didn't sleep. Or November of junior year, when I told my secret email boyfriend I imagine him fantasizing about sex. (Do I remember? Simon. You know I basically stopped breathing until you replied, right?) Or sophomore year, when Ms. Warshauer announced a pop quiz about Chaucer. You told her she was the cause by which you die, and she laughed so hard she had to leave the room for ten minutes.

And then there was ninth grade. Simon, you want to know what I was doing four years ago today? I was stumbling headfirst into the biggest, most all-consuming crush of my fourteen-year-old life. We had biology first period, Ms. Hensel's class, and we were partnered together for the hereditary lab. Do you remember that? It was that truly batshit assignment where we had to flip coins to determine the genotype of our fictional baby. It was the first time we'd ever talked, though I was mostly trying not to openly gape at you.

I remember just how it felt. My rabbit heartbeat, my whirlpool stomach, the way my brain fogged over every time your mouth moved. Of course, I'd noticed you before then. Scrawny freshman Simon Spier, with your moppy hair and thick glasses. You always looked really startled and pleased when anyone talked to you, which was so strange and endearing (Simon, everyone wanted to talk to you. I don't think you've ever understood your own gravitational pull).

So there I was, *making a baby* with this unbearably cute boy (who had all these very strong opinions about coin toss terminology: "How is that a tail, Bram? How? It's the freaking front of the eagle!"). I'll never forget when we had to translate all those genotypes into phenotypes. Our giant-nostriled disaster baby. And, Simon, you loved him. You loved every recessive sprout of hair on his ears. You held my illustration up next to your face, beaming, and it was game over for me, Spier. You've had my heart ever since.

I really wish I could be there tomorrow. I know we'll both be home in five days, but it just sucks. Every moment we miss is so dumbfoundingly hard. And these four stupid years feel like forever. But I plan to be in love with you for so long, Simon Spier. We'll make those four years feel like nothing. Not a blip.

Love,
Blue

FROM: HOURTOHOUR.NOTETONOTE@GMAIL.COM
TO: BLUEGREEN118@GMAIL.COM
DATE: NOV 18 AT 7:12 PM
SUBJECT: I'M STILL JUST . . . HOLY SHIT

Abraham Louis Greenfeld, you are UNBELIEVABLE. I just scrolled back through our emails, and I can't stop smiling. You're such a freaking con artist, you know that? God. Bram. Best fucking surprise of my life. I don't think my feet have even hit the floor yet.

Bram, I'll never get over the sight of you on my bed, cross-legged, in flannel freaking pajama pants, reading a textbook. A TEXTBOOK. Like it's some regular homework night. And I'm just standing in the doorway, fucking *speechless*. Bram, I thought you were a ghost (probably because I'd just come back from a ghost tour, AS YOU KNEW PERFECTLY WELL, BECAUSE YOU'RE IN CAHOOTS WITH MY FREAK-ING ROOMMATE).

Like. I'm just trying to wrap my head around the fact that

you two have been planning this all month. You guys are the sneakiest little sneaks on earth. I still can't believe you SLID INTO KELLAN'S DMs, talked him into bringing me on a ghost tour, and then talked my freaking customs person into *smuggling you into my dorm room*. Such deception!!!! By the way, Kellan and Grover are so fucking pleased with themselves right now. They legit won't stop high-fiving each other (high-fiving! Guys, this is why people think you're a pair of straight dudes!) (okay, so the high fives are a little finger-twiney upon further observation, but STILL).

Anyway, it was perfect. It was just the most perfect birthday imaginable. You're a really great person to be in love with, you know that?

Love,
Simon

FROM: ABBYSUSO710@GMAIL.COM
TO: LEAHONTHEOFFBEAT@GMAIL.COM, SIMONIRVINSPIER
@GMAIL.COM, BRAM.L.GREENFELD@GMAIL.COM,
THEREALNICKEISNER@GMAIL.COM, TEMETTERNICH.HARVARD
@GMAIL.COM, THE.ORIGINAL.ANGEL.BRO@GMAIL.COM
DATE: NOV 23 AT 4:12 PM
SUBJECT: SQUAD THE F UP

Okay, turkey squad, I'm moving this over to email, because apparently *some* people keep missing messages on their Androids (me. Some people is me).

Anyway, clearly tomorrow's the day, so should we lock this in? Want to say noon at Waffle House? Do I really get to see all your gorgeous faces at once????

xoxo,
Abby

FROM: THE.ORIGINAL.ANGEL.BRO@GMAIL.COM
TO: ABBYSUSO710@GMAIL.COM, LEAHONTHEOFFBEAT
@GMAIL.COM, SIMONIRVINSPIER@GMAIL.COM,
BRAM.L.GREENFELD@GMAIL.COM, THEREALNICKEISNER
@GMAIL.COM, TEMETTERNICH.HARVARD@GMAIL.COM

DATE: NOV 23 AT 4:15 PM
SUBJECT: RE: SQUAD THE F UP

Hell yes, all my dudes at Waffle House??? That is a recipe for greatness!

Sent from G-money's iPhone

FROM: THE.ORIGINAL.ANGEL.BRO@GMAIL.COM
TO: ABBYSUSO710@GMAIL.COM, LEAHONTHEOFFBEAT
@GMAIL.COM, SIMONIRVINSPIER@GMAIL.COM,
BRAM.L.GREENFELD@GMAIL.COM, THEREALNICKEISNER
@GMAIL.COM, TEMETTERNICH.HARVARD@GMAIL.COM
DATE: NOV 23 AT 4:17 PM
SUBJECT: RE: SQUAD THE F UP

Wait hold up which Waffle House??

Sent from G-money's iPhone

FROM: SIMONIRVINSPIER@GMAIL.COM
TO: THE.ORIGINAL.ANGEL.BRO@GMAIL.COM, ABBYSUSO710
@GMAIL.COM, LEAHONTHEOFFBEAT@GMAIL.COM,
BRAM.L.GREENFELD@GMAIL.COM, THEREALNICKEISNER
@GMAIL.COM, TEMETTERNICH.HARVARD@GMAIL.COM

DATE: NOV 23 AT 4:21 PM

SUBJECT: RE: SQUAD THE F UP

Roswell Road, right? Near the Starbucks? I'm hyped!!

FROM: THE.ORIGINAL.ANGEL.BRO@GMAIL.COM
TO: SIMONIRVINSPIER@GMAIL.COM, ABBYSUSO710
@GMAIL.COM, LEAHONTHEOFFBEAT@GMAIL.COM,
BRAM.L.GREENFELD@GMAIL.COM, THEREALNICKEISNER
@GMAIL.COM, TEMETTERNICH.HARVARD@GMAIL.COM
DATE: NOV 23 AT 4:23 PM
SUBJECT: RE: SQUAD THE F UP

"WaHo near the Starbucks" LOL, we are most certainly back
in Shady Creek, my friends

Sent from G-money's iPhone

FROM: TEMETTERNICH.HARVARD@GMAIL.COM
TO: THE.ORIGINAL.ANGEL.BRO@GMAIL.COM,
SIMONIRVINSPIER@GMAIL.COM, ABBYSUSO710@GMAIL.COM,
LEAHONTHEOFFBEAT@GMAIL.COM, BRAM.L.GREENFELD
@GMAIL.COM, THEREALNICKEISNER@GMAIL.COM
DATE: NOV 23 AT 4:27 PM
SUBJECT: RE: SQUAD THE F UP

Hi, everyone! So excited for tomorrow. Quick question: "G-money," who are you?

Best,
Taylor

Taylor Eline Metternich
Harvard College
Creekwood High School Salutatorian

FROM: THE.ORIGINAL.ANGEL.BRO@GMAIL.COM
TO: TEMETTERNICH.HARVARD@GMAIL.COM,
SIMONIRVINSPIER@GMAIL.COM, ABBYSUSO710@GMAIL.COM,
LEAHONTHEOFFBEAT@GMAIL.COM, BRAM.L.GREENFELD
@GMAIL.COM, THEREALNICKEISNER@GMAIL.COM
DATE: NOV 23 AT 4:30 PM
SUBJECT: RE: SQUAD THE F UP

'Tis I, Guy Fieri!!
Okay wait, for real, should I bring back the Fieri hair? Do we think the ladies of Tech would appreciate??

Sent from G-money's iPhone

FROM: LEAHONTHEOFFBEAT@GMAIL.COM
TO: THE.ORIGINAL.ANGEL.BRO@GMAIL.COM,

TEMETTERNICH.HARVARD@GMAIL.COM, SIMONIR-
VINSPIER@GMAIL.COM, ABBYSUSO710@GMAIL.COM,
BRAM.L.GREENFELD@GMAIL.COM, THEREALNICKEISNER
@GMAIL.COM
DATE: NOV 23 AT 4:35 PM
SUBJECT: RE: SQUAD THE F UP

Garrett, no.

FROM: ABBYSUSO710@GMAIL.COM
TO: LEAHONTHEOFFBEAT@GMAIL.COM, THE.ORIGINAL
.ANGEL.BRO@GMAIL.COM, TEMETTERNICH.HARVARD
@GMAIL.COM, SIMONIRVINSPIER@GMAIL.COM,
BRAM.L.GREENFELD@GMAIL.COM, THEREALNICKEISNER
@GMAIL.COM
DATE: NOV 23 AT 4:39 PM
SUBJECT: RE: SQUAD THE F UP

Umm, Garrett, what do you mean by "bring back"?
    (Do I want to know??)

FROM: BRAM.L.GREENFELD@GMAIL.COM
TO: ABBYSUSO710@GMAIL.COM, LEAHONTHEOFFBEAT
@GMAIL.COM, THE.ORIGINAL.ANGEL.BRO@GMAIL.COM,
TEMETTERNICH.HARVARD@GMAIL.COM, SIMONIRVINSPIER

58

@GMAIL.COM, THEREALNICKEISNER@GMAIL.COM

DATE: NOV 23 AT 4:44 PM 📎

SUBJECT: RE: SQUAD THE F UP

Fifth grade. Please see attached.

FROM: LEAHONTHEOFFBEAT@GMAIL.COM

TO: ABBYSUSO710@GMAIL.COM

DATE: DEC 10 AT 11:12 PM

SUBJECT: FINALS AND OTHER F-WORDS

Okay, I changed my mind. This is overkill, Abby, you've been at the library for *fifteen hours*. How am I supposed to study for earth science without you tucked up next to me with your knees butterflied out (I maintain that this is not a real sitting position)? Also, hi, how come nobody's randomly initiating a full sequence of dramatic arm and back stretches? Who's going to elbow me in the boobs, Abby? I can't elbow myself.

ABBY SUSO, DO YOU UNDERSTAND THAT I HAVE A PONYTAIL RIGHT NOW, THIS SECOND, AND THERE'S LITERALLY NO ONE DOING LITTLE ABSENTMINDED PIANO MOVES ON THE NAPE OF MY NECK?

So, yeah. I'm officially not a fan of final exams, especially the part where I decide to be an absolute dumbfuck by insisting we hole up in separate library study rooms. I don't know what I was thinking. Let's just quit while we're ahead, okay? We gave it a shot, got a lot of work done, and now we can focus on our anatomy exam, like normal people who don't actually take anatomy.

Real talk: I know how hard you've been working on this story, and I'm amazed by you. Just think, in a few days, it will be done and submitted and well on its way to earning you a big shiny A on your transcript. And then you'll take commissions from your fans, right? How about this one: two girls coming home late for winter break, so they can spend a few extra nights in their dorm room. With the door locked.

Okay, Hermione Granger, I'm shutting down my laptop now. Come home soon. ♥

All best,
LCB

FROM: ABBYSUSO710@GMAIL.COM
TO: LEAHONTHEOFFBEAT@GMAIL.COM
DATE: DEC 9 AT 3:31 AM
SUBJECT: RE: FINALS AND OTHER F-WORDS

I'M DONE, I'M DONE, I'M DONE, THANK GOD. HOLY SHIT. Okay, I'm waiting for the shuttle so I can come home to my little freckle-faced sleeping beauty, and LeLe, I'm so sorry, I know I smell like libraries, but I'll have to shower tomorrow. Because for now, the exhausted void once known as Abigail Suso is passing the fuck out on her silk fucking pillowcase and sleeping in as long as she wants. And then I'm going to wake up tomorrow fully recharged, at which point I'll read this mofo one more time, and then I'm pressing send and turning it in a day before it's due. Yeah, you heard me, I'm going full Taylor Metternich. And then, Leah, then! I'm taking it to the next level with some of that sweet, sweet Analysis of Geometry and Calculus. I am NAILING finals week, Leah, nailing it!!!!!!!

Okay wow, I'm reading this email over, and I know, Leah, I know I sound REALLY drunk. But I'm not. I honestly haven't had a drop to drink (except, like, a billion drops of coffee). I'm just an ungodly level of exhausted right now. And I miss you. I miss your face, LCB. Fuck. I'm so tired, I'm just gonna say the thing, Leah. I love you. I'm in love with you. There it is. (I know this is the least surprising development of all time, and I know I'm not subtle, and I know you're still getting used to that word, but Leah, I love you so much I can't stand it. I think about you constantly. Do you have any idea how often I say your name in my head??)

Anyway, you're going to wake up before me and read this before I'm awake enough to talk my way out of it, and maybe that's a good thing. Or we could just pretend this email never happened. Up to you, Leah Burke. But now you know where I stand.

xo and xo and my whole goddamn heart,
Abby

I am. So jealous. I can't believe I'm still here with an exam Thursday afternoon and three papers due Friday (THREE!) and you've been home for a week. But to answer your questions: I get in Friday afternoon, and Bram should get in thirty minutes after me. We're just going to take MARTA up to the North Creek station, and then Bram's mom is picking us up, so we should be good (but thank you!!!).

And I'm actually here through New Year's! Savannah isn't until January. Sorry, I realize calling it a Chanukah trip was slightly misleading, haha. But yeah, Chanukah's actually over. B and I celebrated when I was in NY after Thanksgiving (he did the menorah prayer in Hebrew, it was so freaking cute). But we're driving down on January 4th so we can do Late Ass Chanukah with his dad, stepmom, Caleb, and various elderly relatives, including Grandpa Greenfeld (who Bram describes as Bernie Sanders meets Eugene Levy, so I'm predicting only excellence).

Okay, so FYI, we're officially confirmed for January 18th for my Top Secret Mission. Right now, the plan is to get him over to Garrett's parents' house after dinner, and we'll have all you guys waiting in the basement. I'm still working on getting a final head count. Nick's already going to be back in Boston (BOOO) and Alice is doing that January winter session thing. But so far, it's me, you and Abby, Garrett, a bunch of the other soccer guys, and obviously Nora. And then we've got Bram's cousin Starr and her boyfriend (they're the ones who wore their school uniforms to Netherworld last year, remember? And you asked them which anime they were cosplaying? ICONIC). Anyway, Bram's cousin SJ on the Greenfeld side is also coming, and we're just waiting for confirmation from SJ's boyfriend. So we're probably looking at around fifteen people or so?

SO, YES, IT'S ALL HAPPENING. Now I just have to keep it a secret from my favorite boy for a month. "G-money" better not blow my cover (I'm still not over it, Leah. Do you think he tells everyone at Tech to call him that? Do you think he tells them that WE call him that?). Also, I'm pretty sure Taylor knows exactly who G-money is, and was just trolling like the legend she is.

Anyway, I'll see you SOON. Come hang with me and Bieber this weekend or something!!

FROM: BLUEGREEN118@GMAIL.COM
TO: HOURTOHOUR.NOTETONOTE@GMAIL.COM
DATE: DEC 31 AT 11:52 PM
SUBJECT: LAST EMAIL OF THE YEAR

Dear Jacques,

You're holding my hand while I write this, which has to be the biggest advantage of being a lefty, and also the best possible reason for one-handed typing. And that's it. That's the email.

> Love,
> Blue

FROM: HOURTOHOUR.NOTETONOTE@GMAIL.COM
TO: BLUEGREEN118@GMAIL.COM
DATE: JAN 1 AT 12:05 AM
SUBJECT: FIRST EMAIL OF THE YEAR

Hello, beautiful boy, you are really something else. You just typed that whole email with one damn hand, didn't you, after *three glasses of champagne*. And not a comma out of place. Not a single freaking error in your whole entire email. Except the part where you say holding hands is the best reason to type one-handed. (Second best, Bram, don't you think? ☺)

Anyway, Drunk Bram, let's go watch the fireworks (and by watch, I mean let's MAKE some fireworks, wink wink wink).

So you're telling me his dad thinks you're back in Atlanta, his mom thinks you're still in Savannah—and you're actually in a hotel room in Macon?? Um. Wow??? Talk about some top-notch divorce-kid trickery. Your boyfriend? Is *diabolically* romantic. Simon, are we sure he's a Ravenclaw? Because that's straight out of the Slytherin playbook. He is the king of surprises, and I'm forced to stan.

Well, Spier, I hope it was absolutely perfect (and I absolutely don't need the details). Can't say I'm surprised about the hotel bumping you to double beds (Georgia's gonna Georgia). But who knows, maybe the front desk took one look at you two and said, nope, these two clearly can't handle the amount of personal space provided by a king bed. Who even wants a king bed?? That's like a long-distance relationship in furniture form.

Anyway, yup! Got back Sunday, classes started yesterday, and it's full steam ahead here. But it's honestly good to be back to the normal routine. Look, I love my mom to the end of the fucking earth, and I'm officially on board with Wells. But if I'm going to have to live with a bunch of blissed-out lovesick dorks, at least one of them better be named Abby Suso.

Okay, hopping on the shuttle now, but keep me posted on party plans. You're going to have to step up your surprise game big-time, Simon Spier, and you know it.

Love,
Leah

P.S. Nope. Don't listen to any of them. Those weren't tears. They were seasonal allergies that powerfully, randomly resurfaced on New Year's. It's a thing.

FROM: SIMONIRVINSPIER@GMAIL.COM

TO: THE.ORIGINAL.ANGEL.BRO@GMAIL.COM, ABBYSUSO710
@GMAIL.COM, LEAHONTHEOFFBEAT@GMAIL.COM

DATE: JAN 16 AT 8:14 PM

SUBJECT: TOP SECRET

NEW STEPPED-UP GAME PLAN FOR FRIDAY, EVERY-
ONE. We're officially scrapping Garrett's house in favor of . . .
you guessed it . . . Operation Ferris Wheel!!

Okay! Here's the info:

Festival doors open at 6:00 p.m. (remember, Perimeter
parking lot, Nordstrom side—you'll see it). So I'm thinking
you guys could get there by 6:30 or so, just to be safe? But you
don't technically have to be in position until 7:00. Leah, I gave
Starr and SJ your number so you can find each other there.
Garrett, you're in charge of looping in the soccer guys. And
then the only other people we're expecting are Nora and Cal (as
friends, FYI, they're NOT back together, and Nora is specifically requesting for us to not "make it weird").

So that means fourteen confirmed (not counting me and
Bram). Luke the ride operator is the MVP, and he's been
prepped, so he knows we need seven adjacent cars. But just in
case, maybe someone wants to run through the plan with him
one more time when you get there?

I'll shoot to have Bram in the ticket line by 7:00, and hopefully at the Ferris wheel by 7:15.

So Luke will let you guys off the ride one car at a time, and—this is so important—the first two people need to act SURPRISED to see us in line. Bram should think we just happened to run into you. But then more and more of you will step off the ride, which is when he'll realize what's happening (and I'm calling it, he's going to do his cute little eye-flare-quick-inhale surprised face, and I CAN'T WAIT).

And then Bram and I get on the ride, I press play on Otis Redding, and we're off!

Sound good to everyone??

FROM: THE.ORIGINAL.ANGEL.BRO@GMAIL.COM
TO: SIMONIRVINSPIER@GMAIL.COM, ABBYSUSO710
@GMAIL.COM, LEAHONTHEOFFBEAT@GMAIL.COM
DATE: JAN 16 AT 8:31 PM
SUBJECT: RE: TOP SECRET

Spier, gotta be honest, this is the most intense email I've ever read, and that includes my conspiracy theorist uncle *and* Greenfeld during finals week.

Deep breaths, friend!!!

Sent from G-money's iPhone

FROM: ABBYSUSO710@GMAIL.COM
TO: THE.ORIGINAL.ANGEL.BRO@GMAIL.COM,
SIMONIRVINSPIER@GMAIL.COM, LEAHONTHEOFFBEAT
@GMAIL.COM
DATE: JAN 16 AT 8:40 PM
SUBJECT: RE: TOP SECRET

I LOVE IT!!! He is going to lose his shit (but in his cute little self-contained Bram way, I can't wait). Simon, you're a genius.

FROM: LEAHONTHEOFFBEAT@GMAIL.COM
TO: ABBYSUSO710@GMAIL.COM
DATE: JAN 16 AT 8:48 PM
SUBJECT: RE: TOP SECRET

Legit can't stop laughing at G-money calling out *Bram* for sending intense emails during finals week. Has he met you?

FROM: ABBYSUSO710@GMAIL.COM
TO: LEAHONTHEOFFBEAT@GMAIL.COM
DATE: JAN 16 AT 8:50 PM
SUBJECT: RE: TOP SECRET

WELL, AREN'T YOU FUNNY.

FROM: LEAHONTHEOFFBEAT@GMAIL.COM

TO: ABBYSUSO710@GMAIL.COM, THE.ORIGINAL.ANGEL
.BRO@GMAIL.COM, SIMONIRVINSPIER@GMAIL.COM

DATE: JAN 16 AT 8:55 PM

SUBJECT: RE: TOP SECRET

Agreed, Simon. This may actually be Greenfeld-worthy.

Just confirming: We are indeed planning to make it weird for Nora, right?

FROM: SIMONIRVINSPIER@GMAIL.COM

TO: LEAHONTHEOFFBEAT@GMAIL.COM, ABBYSUSO710
@GMAIL.COM, THE.ORIGINAL.ANGEL.BRO@GMAIL.COM

DATE: JAN 16 AT 9:06 PM

SUBJECT: RE: TOP SECRET

Oh, we are *absolutely* making it weird for Nora.

FROM: ABBYSUSO710@GMAIL.COM

TO: SIMONIRVINSPIER@GMAIL.COM, LEAHONTHEOFFBEAT
@GMAIL.COM, THE.ORIGINAL.ANGEL.BRO@GMAIL.COM

DATE: JAN 16 AT 9:10 PM

SUBJECT: RE: TOP SECRET

Okay, one question, Si. I know your guy Luke is up to speed

and ready to go, but . . . Simon, are we 100 percent sure he's on duty Friday? Should we have a backup plan lined up?

FROM: SIMONIRVINSPIER@GMAIL.COM
TO: ABBYSUSO710@GMAIL.COM, LEAHONTHEOFFBEAT
@GMAIL.COM, THE.ORIGINAL.ANGEL.BRO@GMAIL.COM
DATE: JAN 16 AT 9:15 PM
SUBJECT: RE: TOP SECRET

We don't need a backup plan. ☺ Let's just say Luke is taking this VERY seriously.

FROM: LEAHONTHEOFFBEAT@GMAIL.COM
TO: SIMONIRVINSPIER@GMAIL.COM, ABBYSUSO710
@GMAIL.COM, THE.ORIGINAL.ANGEL.BRO
@GMAIL.COM
DATE: JAN 16 AT 9:18 PM
SUBJECT: RE: TOP SECRET

Simon . . . please tell me we aren't Martin Addisoning the Ferris wheel operator.

FROM: SIMONIRVINSPIER@GMAIL.COM
TO: LEAHONTHEOFFBEAT@GMAIL.COM, ABBYSUSO710
@GMAIL.COM, THE.ORIGINAL.ANGEL.BRO@GMAIL.COM

DATE: JAN 16 AT 9:21 PM
SUBJECT: RE: TOP SECRET

WTF, LEAH NO, WE ARE NOT MARTIN ADDISONING THE FERRIS WHEEL OPERATOR!!! Have you considered that maybe Luke just happens to be a nice guy who likes birthdays and wants to help me surprise my boyfriend??

FROM: LEAHONTHEOFFBEAT@GMAIL.COM
TO: SIMONIRVINSPIER@GMAIL.COM, ABBYSUSO710 @GMAIL.COM, THE.ORIGINAL.ANGEL.BRO@GMAIL.COM
DATE: JAN 16 AT 9:23 PM
SUBJECT: RE: TOP SECRET

Nope, no one likes birthdays that much.

FROM: SIMONIRVINSPIER@GMAIL.COM
TO: LEAHONTHEOFFBEAT@GMAIL.COM, ABBYSUSO710 @GMAIL.COM, THE.ORIGINAL.ANGEL.BRO@GMAIL.COM
DATE: JAN 16 AT 9:26 PM
SUBJECT: RE: TOP SECRET

Which is why I told Luke it's a marriage proposal. ☺

FROM: LEAHONTHEOFFBEAT@GMAIL.COM

TO: SIMONIRVINSPIER@GMAIL.COM, ABBYSUSO710
@GMAIL.COM, THE.ORIGINAL.ANGEL.BRO@GMAIL.COM
DATE: JAN 16 AT 9:27 PM
SUBJECT: RE: TOP SECRET

SIMON, NO, THIS IS A VERY BAD IDEA!!!!!!!!!

FROM: LEAHONTHEOFFBEAT@GMAIL.COM
TO: ABBYSUSO710@GMAIL.COM
DATE: JAN 16 AT 9:28 PM
SUBJECT: RE: TOP SECRET

OH GOD

FROM: ABBYSUSO710@GMAIL.COM
TO: LEAHONTHEOFFBEAT@GMAIL.COM
DATE: JAN 16 AT 9:30 PM
SUBJECT: RE: TOP SECRET

I KNOW, LEAH, I KNOW, AND I AM UTTERLY SPEECH-
LESS

FROM: THE.ORIGINAL.ANGEL.BRO@GMAIL.COM
TO: LEAHONTHEOFFBEAT@GMAIL.COM, SIMONIRVIN-
SPIER@GMAIL.COM, ABBYSUSO710@GMAIL.COM

75

DATE: JAN 16 AT 9:31 PM
SUBJECT: RE: TOP SECRET

NO FUCKING WAY. Like for real? You guys are getting engaged?? Holy shit Spier, congrats!!!!!

Sent from G-money's iPhone

FROM: SIMONIRVINSPIER@GMAIL.COM
TO: THE.ORIGINAL.ANGEL.BRO@GMAIL.COM,
LEAHONTHEOFFBEAT@GMAIL.COM, ABBYSUSO710
@GMAIL.COM
DATE: JAN 16 AT 9:35 PM
SUBJECT: RE: TOP SECRET

Garrett, no!!!! OMG, I'm not actually proposing to Bram on Friday! Oh my god, I'm laughing so hard right now. Garrett, I'm nineteen, I literally don't eat vegetables yet. LOL, NOT proposing. I just *told* Luke I'm proposing, so he'll take the plan seriously.

Glad I could clear that up!!! WOW.

FROM: ABBYSUSO710@GMAIL.COM
TO: LEAHONTHEOFFBEAT@GMAIL.COM
DATE: JAN 16 AT 9:39 PM
SUBJECT: RE: TOP SECRET

This conversation. Is BANANAS.

I'm making popcorn.

FROM: LEAHONTHEOFFBEAT@GMAIL.COM

TO: ABBYSUSO710@GMAIL.COM

DATE: JAN 16 AT 9:41 PM

SUBJECT: RE: TOP SECRET

God. What a time to be alive.

All right, wish me luck, I'm going in.

FROM: LEAHONTHEOFFBEAT@GMAIL.COM

TO: SIMONIRVINSPIER@GMAIL.COM

DATE: JAN 16 AT 9:53 PM

SUBJECT: RE: TOP SECRET

Okay, Simon, I need you to listen to me when I tell you THIS IS NOT A GOOD IDEA. Letting people think you're proposing to Bram is *not a good idea.* Si, what do you think's going to happen when you and Bram step off the Ferris wheel? Is your pal Luke going to wish Bram a happy birthday? No, he's going to congratulate you on your engagement. And every single person in line? Is going to congratulate you on your engagement.

You know what Bram's going to think, right? He's going to think you got on that Ferris wheel planning to ask him to marry you.

So put yourself in his head for a second. What if you thought Bram was trying to propose to you? Let's say you had reason to believe he almost asked you but lost his nerve at the last second.

You'd be asking yourself so many questions, right? Is he the person you want to spend your life with? Your whole life, Simon. Do you want to have sex with him for seventy years? Do you want to change diapers and file taxes and buy health insurance with him? Do you feel like you can even know that right now? And if he's the one, Simon, do you actually want to do this when you're nineteen? You have to understand that Bram's going to be asking himself all these things.

And Simon, say Bram decides yeah, I'm all in. He'll either be freaking the fuck out, 24/7, waiting for you to actually ask him, or he's going to turn around and do it himself. Are you ready to be proposed to? Do you know how you'd answer?

I'm sorry, Si, I'm not trying to freak you out. But I get the sense you two are really serious about each other, which means this isn't just some thought exercise. It's not something to play around with. I know that's not your intention, of course, but make sure you're thinking everything through, okay? Be careful with your heart, and his.

Look, I'm not worried about tomorrow. I can explain everything to Luke before you get there, and we'll nip this in the bud. But . . . maybe you and Bram should talk about this stuff at some point? I don't know, maybe you already have. And to be clear, I don't think most nineteen-year-old couples need to bring this shit into the room *anytime* soon.

But I think maybe you guys do.

Simon, why don't you start with this question for yourself: What made you think of telling Luke this was a marriage proposal? Don't tell me it's so he'd take the birthday surprise seriously, I get that. But why a *marriage proposal*?

And how did it feel when you said it out loud?

Dear Jacques,

Just think: In four months, we'll be home again, with the whole summer ahead of us, and none of this will feel real. This semester won't even leave a mark, Simon. It'll be like some story we heard two years ago.

I can't wait to forget what missing you feels like.

Well. You're officially on a plane, and I've got about an hour left until mine boards. The goodbye hasn't really hit me yet. It feels like maybe you're in the bathroom, or buying overpriced breath mints (mints that I won't get to experience secondhand) (okay, now it's starting to hit me).

You know what I hate about endings? The way they always feel like we made some tactical error. Like time only passed because we let it. Can you believe I'm out here regretting the end of January, like it was my choice?

I keep thinking about what Nick said on New Year's about video game save points. Our little philosopher. I forgot how much sense he makes sometimes (even more so when I've had champagne, apparently). I can't remember how much of that discussion you were there for (I think this was when you were upstairs FaceTiming Kellan and Grover). But I'll try to walk you through the context.

Okay, so this was about one or two in the morning, and Taylor was relentlessly trying to make a singalong happen. But everyone was pretty lukewarm about it (except Leah, who was *emphatically* disinterested), so Taylor just started singing by herself. And it was one of those moments, Simon. You want to roll your eyes, because it's Taylor, but her voice kind of stopped us all in our tracks. It was that song "More Than Words" (I think it's on your Amtrak shuffle playlist, right?). Anyway, Nick jumped in and started playing it on his guitar and doing this really quiet vocal harmony, and I think we were all a little spellbound. And as soon as it was over, Leah jumped up and ran to the bathroom. Obviously, Abby went after her, and they were both a little red-eyed when they came back. So Taylor asked if they were okay, and Abby smiled and said, "I just wish I could freeze this moment."

So Nick just kind of stared at them for a minute, and I felt so nauseated, Simon. Because I really thought Nick was in a good place about the whole Abby and Leah thing, but of course I started second-guessing everything. Like, I actually flinched a little when Nick opened his mouth, because I was so sure he was going to say something awkward. But he got this faraway look on his face, and started talking about time and memory.

And that's when you walked in, but I don't know if you caught what he was saying.

It was basically this: When we say we want to freeze time, what we mean is that we want to control our memories. We want to choose which moments we'll keep forever. We want to guarantee the best ones won't slip away from us somehow. So when something beautiful happens, there's this impulse to press pause and save the game. We want to make sure we can find our way back to that moment.

Simon, you want to know the moment I'd choose for my save point? Last Friday, top of the Ferris wheel. Specifically, the part where you caught me staring at the Tilt-A-Whirl and decided to destroy me with two words.

Can we keep that one? Can we please go back there?

Love,
Blue

FROM: HOURTOHOUR.NOTETONOTE@GMAIL.COM
TO: BLUEGREEN118@GMAIL.COM
DATE: JAN 25 AT 10:41 AM
SUBJECT: I KNOW I'M LATE.

Dear Blue,

Well, here it is: our two-year anniversary. So glad we get to spend it a million fucking miles away from each other. Just like we'll be spending Valentine's Day a million fucking miles away from each other.

I didn't think it could get harder. I guess I thought I'd be used to this? Nope, looks like the only thing I got used to is seeing you every day for winter break. And now you're gone, and I feel almost decapitated. Like my brain and my body have nothing to do with each other. I keep showing up at class and forgetting the part where I walked there. Or Kellan will say my name, and then I find out it's the tenth time he's said it.

Bram, it's freaking me out. I feel like it's not even me in my head. I keep thinking about this email Leah sent me over break (which of course I never replied to, because I'm an asshole). I don't even know what to say about it, B, but different parts of it keep hitting me out of nowhere. Sorry I'm sitting here basically subtweeting someone else's email. And being a general mopehead. I'll stop. I'm stopping now. I'm moving on to something happy. Or sad-happy, I guess.

So I've been thinking about what I'd pick for my save point. (By the way, I absolutely remember Nick saying this, and for what it's worth, you explained it all much more poetically. I'm pretty sure Nick used the word "respawning.")

Anyway, my first thought was the winter carnival (junior year edition). But then I was like, what about the Publix parking lot? Or senior year homecoming? ☺ Or my birthday. Or

Macon. Or last Friday. It's a LOT. And Bram, you know how I am about choices.

But here's where I landed: I pick now. Like right here in my dorm room, in my golden retriever pajama pants, emailing you from 117 and 1/2 miles away. Because whether I like it or not, my today brain is the only one that has our whole story. I mean, it's the exact same reason Deathly Hallows is my desert island book. All the other books are right there tucked away inside it.

Bram, I'll take every single shitty memory without you, if it means I get to keep the whole nesting doll.

Happy anniversary, B.

Love,
(Here you go, I'm doing this just for you, you dork.)
Jacques

Hey! Sorry it took me a second to sit down and write back to this. Just wanted to thank you and Abby again for checking in on me (your voice memo was so freaking cute)! But seriously, I'm totally fine! Just pretty much getting back into the swing of things. Kellan and Grover have been in Annapolis all weekend for early Valentine's Day, so I've had the room to myself! They should be back any minute, though, assuming they weren't overly haunted by any "ghostly entities" from their bed-and-breakfast. (Okay, but serious question: If the ghostly entity never shows up, does that mean it . . . ghosted them??)

Other than that, it's just business as usual, and classes are busy but good!! Unfortunately, my enemy from Intro Psych who doesn't know he's my enemy is now continuing his reign of terror and misogyny in Research Methods and Stats. But he got his ass handed to him during lab last week by this really soft-spoken nonbinary kid named Skyler, and it was all so beautiful to watch!

Oh my god, Leah, I can't believe the size of your classes!!

I can't even fathom it. Is it overwhelming going to school with that many people? I wonder about that sometimes. Do you end up mostly running into the same people, or is it just kind of big and sprawling? I guess in a way, it would be like living in a big city or something? I don't know. I'm just curious. And is it easier since Abby's there?

But I do feel like I'm finally getting to know people here!! My customs group has been doing lots of game nights lately (they're really into Taboo—which would be amazing, except I'm SO much better at it when I play with you guys!). And I'm kind of an a cappella groupie now! Not really, I've just been helping them with their website, but it's been so cool, and I've gotten to sit in on some of their rehearsals (it's this all-girl group called the Outskirts, and two of my hallmates are in it, and they're SO GOOD, Leah. Look them up. They're on YouTube)!

Not much planned for Valentine's Day—I think we're probably just going to eat dinner in our rooms and FaceTime! What about you (i.e., what has Abby talked you into so far)?

Anyway, it was really good to talk to you the other day, and I'm sorry again that I've been so off the grid lately!! And tell Abby I'll reply to her soon, I promise, but also you can share this email with her if you want so she knows I'm fine! Okay, I love and miss you guys a lot!!!!

FROM: LEAHONTHEOFFBEAT@GMAIL.COM
TO: ABBYSUSO710@GMAIL.COM
DATE: FEB 11 AT 10:04 AM
SUBJECT: FWD: RE: EVERYTHING GOOD?

Yeah, I'm pretty fucking concerned, actually. Like, that is . . . an aggressively upbeat email. And I'm impressed that he managed to use infinity exclamation points, but . . . I'm not really buying the whole everything's-fine-here schtick?

I don't know, maybe I'm overreacting. Do we think this is just chaotic Simon being chaotic? Or is this chaotic depressed Simon in the midst of an unprecedented downward spiral, the depths of which he is both unable and, for some reason, unwilling to fully communicate?? I swear to god. SIMON, YOU KNOW EVERY WORD TO EVERY GODDAMN ELLIOTT SMITH SONG. How is it *this hard* for him to talk about sadness?

And he still hasn't replied to the other email, of course, but it's not even just that. It's the fact that he hasn't even *acknowledged* it, other than thanking me for handling things with the ride operator. But nothing since then, Abby. He hasn't even mentioned it in a text. It's kind of freaking me out. He's normally so open with me.

Abby, what do we do??

FROM: ABBYSUSO710@GMAIL.COM

TO: LEAHONTHEOFFBEAT@GMAIL.COM

DATE: FEB 11 AT 10:24 AM

SUBJECT: RE: FWD: RE: EVERYTHING GOOD?

Hold up, getting my fake Word document into position . . . wait for it . . . and . . .

Okay! So yeah, Simon's definitely NOT giving off the chill vibes he thinks he is, but I also don't know that we're in "unprecedented downward spiral" territory? LOL. I think he's just missing Bram a lot, and maybe trying to distract himself and stay positive. And I guess he's trying to keep us from worrying about him (and yeah, it probably would have landed better with about twenty fewer exclamation points, but Simon's pretty exclaim-y in general, don't you think?).

But I get why you're worried. And I get the impression it's less about this particular Simon-on-crack email (god, the *ghost pun*), and more about the email he hasn't replied to. I'm reading between the lines a little, maybe, but Leah . . . you don't feel like you pushed Simon into an unprecedented downward spiral, right? I don't care what you wrote in that email. If Simon's depressed or spiraling or confused right now, that's because of whatever chemical or situational stuff he's dealing with. Maybe both! And yeah, I think it's a good idea to keep checking in on him, but don't let this haunt you, okay (or "overly haunt" you—wtf does that even mean, Simon? Is there some known acceptable haunting level? SMDH, truly, what are we going to do with that boy??).

Okay, shifting gears for a second, because as you may have noticed, it's February 11th, which means you and I desperately need to talk about the big VD (NOT the big venereal disease, Burke, don't even try me). So here's the deal, my cynical misanthrope of a girlfriend: I hereby challenge you to a single round of Valentine Cliché Bingo.

The rules are as follows:

On February 13th, each participant will work privately to create one (1) traditionally structured Bingo card, featuring five rows and five columns, for a total of twenty-five squares. Then (with the exception of the Free Space in the center) participants will fill in each square with a written description of one Valentine's Day cliché. This may be a gift, tradition, activity, or phrase (for example: "a dozen red roses," "candlelit dinner," "be my valentine," etc.). All twenty-four squares must contain different clichés, and the items will be chosen and arranged at the participant's discretion.

THE PARTICIPANTS MUST REFRAIN FROM REVEALING THEIR BINGO CARDS TO EACH OTHER FOR THE ENTIRE DURATION OF THE GAME. THIS IS OF CRITICAL, MONUMENTAL IMPORTANCE.

On February 14th, beginning at 8:00 a.m. EST, the participants (with no knowledge of the twenty-four items listed on each other's Bingo cards) will engage in Valentine-themed

clichés for the duration of the day. The goal for both participants will be to engage in a cliché listed on the *other* participant's
Bingo card.

If a participant enacts a cliché listed on the other participant's card, the cardholder MUST mark off the item as
complete. (So, for example, if Participant A's square reads "a
dozen red roses," and Participant L presents Participant A, in
real life, with a dozen red roses? Participant A *must* mark off
that square on her Bingo card).

If either participant marks off five squares in a row, in any
orientation (vertical, horizontal, or diagonal), this means the
OTHER participant has successfully achieved Bingo. The
cardholder must immediately notify the other participant of
her Bingo status, thus ending the game.

So here's the deal: If you win, I'll agree to make precisely
zero Valentine's Day–themed posts on social media for the
entire day. But, Leah, if I win? You're posting a picture of every
fucking teddy bear and piece of chocolate I give you.

So, Valentine, do you accept these terms?

(God, I can't wait to watch Competitive Leah and Cliché-
Avoidance Leah war it out all over your beautiful face.)

xoxo,
Abby

FROM: HOURTOHOUR.NOTETONOTE@GMAIL.COM

TO: BLUEGREEN118@GMAIL.COM

DATE: FEB 15 AT 9:13 PM

SUBJECT: RE: DID YOU SEE THIS?

RIGHT??? IT'S SO WEIRD. Do you think she got hacked?? Or possessed? Don't get me wrong, it's pretty freaking cute, but Leah Burke Instagramming her Valentine's Day haul is the freshman year plot twist I didn't see coming.

Anyway, I'm fine. It just sucked doing Valentine's Day over FaceTime. Which is ridiculous, because I don't even care that much about Valentine's Day! Being apart on our anniversary was definitely worse. But it's all kind of cumulative, I guess. I just miss you on top of missing you on top of missing you.

But I'm trying SO hard. I had a snowball fight with both Jacobs, and I've crashed every single one of Rachel and Liza's a cappella rehearsals. I've been grabbing lunch after psych every day with Skyler. I'm watching every weird fucking horror movie Kellan puts on, and I'm playing violent video games with Jocelyn (even though she keeps killing me right when I respawn, she's so ruthless). I guess it all seems so trivial when I write it out like that. But I don't really know what else to do. If I'm going to be here, I should try to be here, you know? I have to let it be my real life.

I don't know, B. I guess I'm figuring some stuff out.

But Bram, I want to know everything you're up to. I want to know if you're making snowmen, and stargazing, and eating barbecued dinosaurs, and watching weird performance art with Ella and Miriam, and befriending more makeup gurus. I want you to tell me every detail of your soccer games so I can nod along and pretend I understand what scrimmages and corner kicks are. Just be happy, okay? I want you to miss me, and think about me, and be in love with me, and be happy.

FROM: BLUEGREEN118@GMAIL.COM
TO: HOURTOHOUR.NOTETONOTE@GMAIL.COM
DATE: FEB 16 AT 11:10 AM
SUBJECT: RE: DID YOU SEE THIS?

Dear Jacques,

You know, I always forget your emails have the ability to take my breath away.

I'm so bewildered by it. It's just symbols and white space, and it's affecting my basic biological functions. I think your keyboard must have some kind of direct link to my brain.

That last sentence.

Simon, let me be clear: I miss you. I think about you. I'm

in love with you. Happiness is a shifting variable, but those are my constants.

I think you're right to carve out a Real Life at school. That's the healthy thing, right? I'm trying, too, though I don't know if my Real Life is as exciting as you're imagining. No snowmen so far, and I don't know that stargazing is a thing in Manhattan. ☺ But I'm hanging out a lot with Ella and Miriam, and they are most certainly roping me into ALL the weird performance art. I don't know if I'd say I've *befriended* Alec, but we've grabbed dinner a few times, and he keeps offering to do my makeup. Simon, how do I tell a beauty guru with half a million followers that I'm into makeup like the Pentecostal Church is into makeup? But I bet he'll give you Troye Sivan eyes when you're here in March, if you want (I promise I'll wear my soccer knee socks for you if you do). You know everyone here is desperate to meet you, right?

And I don't know what you're figuring out, Simon, but if you ever need to talk it through, I'm all yours. But you know that.

And I miss you on top of missing you on top of missing you too.

Love,
Blue

Abby, I'm a DISASTER—I can't believe I'm writing back to you a month late. I know. I know we've texted and WhatsApped a zillion times since then, but ugh, I'm still so sorry. And here you had so many really lovely questions for me that are all wildly out of date. But in case you're for some reason still wondering: The rest of winter break was really good! Bram and I mostly just holed up at his mom's house (strategic avoidance of the famous Jack and Emily Spier mortification two-punch). I did get back to Philadelphia safely on January 22nd. ☺ And yup, I know what I'm taking this semester (probably a good thing, seeing as the semester's almost halfway over at this point, because I'm a jerk who takes a month to answer basic freaking questions).

Anyway, I'm on a train!! To New York!!! And I'm staying for a full week, during which I will be an EXEMPLAR of independence and self-restraint as Bram conquers midterms. And then he's coming back with me to Philly. I'M SO HAPPY RIGHT NOW, ABBY. Every time anyone looks at me, I start smiling (and for the record, if you ever want a bunch of northerners to give you *lots* of extra space on a train, that's the way to do it).

But you guys have early spring break like me, right? When do you leave for DC? I'm so excited Leah's coming with you!! This will be her first time meeting the twins, right? And Xavier? I know Nick enjoyed meeting them (except the part where your cousin Cassie threatened to disembowel him if he ever hurt you. Apparently she was very convincing?). Okay, I'm guessing you don't need recommendations for stuff to do, but Kellan wants me to tell you there are some really good Edgar Allan Poe attractions in Baltimore. So if you're in the mood for learning about Edgar Allan Poe and driving up to Baltimore, there's . . . that?

Okay, pulling into Penn Station! Safest travels to you guys, and please send lots of pics, and say hi to the Obamas for me if you see them??

Love,
Simon

FROM: SIMONIRVINSPIER@GMAIL.COM

TO: THE.ORIGINAL.ANGEL.BRO@GMAIL.COM, ABBYSUSO710
@GMAIL.COM, LEAHONTHEOFFBEAT@GMAIL.COM,
BRAM.L.GREENFELD@GMAIL.COM, THEREALNICKEISNER
@GMAIL.COM, TEMETTERNICH.HARVARD@GMAIL.COM

DATE: MAR 11 AT 8:39 AM

SUBJECT: BIG APPLE SHENANIGANS

So . . . I was going make a vlog for you guys, but there were profound technical difficulties (i.e., I woke up with what one might call a "Big Apple"–sized zit). But alas, onward! I am switching this spectacle over to the group email chain, and guys, City Boy Spier is about to take you on the tour of a lifetime. ARE YOU READY?

FROM: LEAHONTHEOFFBEAT@GMAIL.COM

TO: SIMONIRVINSPIER@GMAIL.COM, THE.ORIGINAL
.ANGEL.BRO@GMAIL.COM, ABBYSUSO710@GMAIL.COM,
BRAM.L.GREENFELD@GMAIL.COM, THEREALNICKEISNER
@GMAIL.COM, TEMETTERNICH.HARVARD@GMAIL.COM

DATE: MAR 11 AT 8:48 AM

SUBJECT: RE: BIG APPLE SHENANIGANS

Bram kicked you out so he could study for finals, didn't he?

FROM: SIMONIRVINSPIER@GMAIL.COM

TO: LEAHONTHEOFFBEAT@GMAIL.COM, THE.ORIGINAL
.ANGEL.BRO@GMAIL.COM, ABBYSUSO710@GMAIL.COM,
BRAM.L.GREENFELD@GMAIL.COM, THEREALNICKEISNER
@GMAIL.COM, TEMETTERNICH.HARVARD@GMAIL.COM

DATE: MAR 11 AT 8:52 AM

SUBJECT: RE: BIG APPLE SHENANIGANS

My reasons for embarking on this adventure are of little importance. Alas, the journey begins!!!

First stop, as you see, is an extremely grand church on the
Upper West Side, which may in fact actually be Hogwarts. But I'm
afraid I can't confirm this, seeing as it doesn't open until nine. Alas,
I am attaching a photo of the exterior and heading to the subway,
where the journey must continue.

FROM: LEAHONTHEOFFBEAT@GMAIL.COM

TO: SIMONIRVINSPIER@GMAIL.COM, THE.ORIGINAL
.ANGEL.BRO@GMAIL.COM, ABBYSUSO710@GMAIL.COM,
BRAM.L.GREENFELD@GMAIL.COM, THEREALNICKEISNER
@GMAIL.COM, TEMETTERNICH.HARVARD@GMAIL.COM

DATE: MAR 11 AT 8:59 AM

SUBJECT: RE: BIG APPLE SHENANIGANS

You . . . realize you sent that email at 8:52, right?

FROM: THE.ORIGINAL.ANGEL.BRO@GMAIL.COM
TO: LEAHONTHEOFFBEAT@GMAIL.COM, SIMONIRVINSPIER
@GMAIL.COM, ABBYSUSO710@GMAIL.COM, BRAM.L
.GREENFELD@GMAIL.COM, THEREALNICKEISNER@GMAIL
.COM, TEMETTERNICH.HARVARD@GMAIL.COM
DATE: MAR 11 AT 9:15 AM
SUBJECT: RE: BIG APPLE SHENANIGANS

Okay gang, who's in charge of counting how many times Spier says "alas"??

Sent from G-money's iPhone

FROM: SIMONIRVINSPIER@GMAIL.COM
TO: THE.ORIGINAL.ANGEL.BRO@GMAIL.COM,
LEAHONTHEOFFBEAT@GMAIL.COM, ABBYSUSO710
@GMAIL.COM, BRAM.L.GREENFELD@GMAIL.COM,
THEREALNICKEISNER@GMAIL.COM, TEMETTERNICH
.HARVARD@GMAIL.COM
DATE: MAR 11 AT 9:46 AM
SUBJECT: RE: BIG APPLE SHENANIGANS

ALAS. Next stop is the most delicious smelling place my nose has ever experienced, the famous Levain Bakery. I have just procured a dark chocolate chocolate-chip cookie (which, per my extensive research, is the most desirable flavor). I have also procured a dark chocolate peanut-butter chip cookie, for Bram-related reasons. I will now photograph the dark chocolate chocolate-chip cookie (see attached), and will report back momentarily on its flavor.

And . . . I am delighted to report that my research is absolutely fucking correct. Folks, this is Oreo-level greatness.

FROM: LEAHONTHEOFFBEAT@GMAIL.COM
TO: SIMONIRVINSPIER@GMAIL.COM, THE.ORIGINAL
.ANGEL.BRO@GMAIL.COM, ABBYSUSO710@GMAIL.COM,
BRAM.L.GREENFELD@GMAIL.COM, THEREALNICKEISNER
@GMAIL.COM, TEMETTERNICH.HARVARD@GMAIL.COM
DATE: MAR 11 AT 10:19 AM
SUBJECT: RE: BIG APPLE SHENANIGANS

And by "extensive research," you mean you saw it in a young adult novel, right?

FROM: SIMONIRVINSPIER@GMAIL.COM
TO: THE.ORIGINAL.ANGEL.BRO@GMAIL.COM,
LEAHONTHEOFFBEAT@GMAIL.COM, ABBYSUSO710
@GMAIL.COM, BRAM.L.GREENFELD@GMAIL.COM,
THEREALNICKEISNER@GMAIL.COM, TEMETTERNICH
.HARVARD@GMAIL.COM

It was a very thick young adult novel.

FROM: TEMETTERNICH.HARVARD@GMAIL.COM

TO: SIMONIRVINSPIER@GMAIL.COM, THE.ORIGINAL
.ANGEL.BRO@GMAIL.COM, LEAHONTHEOFFBEAT@GMAIL
.COM, ABBYSUSO710@GMAIL.COM, BRAM.L.GREENFELD
@GMAIL.COM, THEREALNICKEISNER@GMAIL.COM,

DATE: MAR 11 AT 10:28 AM

SUBJECT: RE: BIG APPLE SHENANIGANS

Simon, I'm loving these updates!! The Cathedral Church of
Saint John the Divine is so beautiful, isn't it? I actually think
it's one of my top five cathedrals, and certainly my favorite one
in the States. If you get a chance, you should definitely see le
Mont-Saint-Michel in la Normandie, but I can give you other
recommendations too.

And that cookie looks delicious. ☺ Wish I still had my high
school metabolism.

Taylor Eline Metternich
Harvard College
Creekwood High School Salutatorian

FROM: LEAHONTHEOFFBEAT@GMAIL.COM
TO: ABBYSUSO710@GMAIL.COM
DATE: MAR 11 AT 10:32 AM
SUBJECT: RE: BIG APPLE SHENANIGANS

She did not just fucking mention her metabolism . . .

FROM: SIMONIRVINSPIER@GMAIL.COM
TO: TEMETTERNICH.HARVARD@GMAIL.COM, THE.ORIGINAL
.ANGEL.BRO@GMAIL.COM, LEAHONTHEOFFBEAT@GMAIL
.COM, ABBYSUSO710@GMAIL.COM, BRAM.L.GREENFELD
@GMAIL.COM, THEREALNICKEISNER@GMAIL.COM
DATE: MAR 11 AT 11:49 AM ✐
SUBJECT: RE: BIG APPLE SHENANIGANS

Thank you, Taylor, and I will certainly consider it if I'm ever looking for a cathedral that's in France as opposed to a six-minute walk from my boyfriend's dorm room.

So, here (see attached) we have the Lyric Theatre, home of *Harry Potter and the Cursed Child*, which I will unfortunately only be appreciating from the outside for this trip. But, alas, City Boy Spier will most certainly be back one day!!

(Side note: Can I just say I'm REALLY freaking loving this? I don't think I've ever really just explored New York before, and it's honestly such a quality city?? Five stars.)

FROM: THEREALNICKEISNER@GMAIL.COM

TO: SIMONIRVINSPIER@GMAIL.COM, TEMETTERNICH
.HARVARD@GMAIL.COM, THE.ORIGINAL.ANGEL.BRO
@GMAIL.COM, LEAHONTHEOFFBEAT@GMAIL.COM,
ABBYSUSO710@GMAIL.COM, BRAM.L.GREENFELD@GMAIL
.COM

DATE: MAR 11 AT 11:56 AM

SUBJECT: RE: BIG APPLE SHENANIGANS

Five stars from Simon Spier?? Guess I better keep this little
town on my radar.

FROM: THE.ORIGINAL.ANGEL.BRO@GMAIL.COM

TO: THEREALNICKEISNER@GMAIL.COM,
LEAHONTHEOFFBEAT@GMAIL.COM, SIMONIRVINSPIER
@GMAIL.COM, ABBYSUSO710@GMAIL.COM, BRAM.L
.GREENFELD@GMAIL.COM, TEMETTERNICH.HARVARD
@GMAIL.COM

DATE: MAR 11 AT 1:51 PM

SUBJECT: RE: BIG APPLE SHENANIGANS

So now you're just going to leave us hanging, City Boy Spier??
What's our next tour stop?

Sent from G-money's iPhone

FROM: SIMONIRVINSPIER@GMAIL.COM

TO: THE.ORIGINAL.ANGEL.BRO@GMAIL.COM,
TEMETTERNICH.HARVARD@GMAIL.COM, LEAHONTHEOFFBEAT
@GMAIL.COM, ABBYSUSO710@GMAIL.COM, BRAM.L
.GREENFELD@GMAIL.COM, THEREALNICKEISNER@GMAIL
.COM

DATE: MAR 11 AT 2:05 PM

SUBJECT: RE: BIG APPLE SHENANIGANS

Oops—just looking at some stuff in Greenwich Village. Look, it's Washington Square Park!!!

FROM: LEAHONTHEOFFBEAT@GMAIL.COM

TO: ABBYSUSO710@GMAIL.COM

DATE: MAR 11 AT 2:07 PM

SUBJECT: RE: BIG APPLE SHENANIGANS

Washington Square Park. Interesting . . .

FROM: ABBYSUSO710@GMAIL.COM

TO: LEAHONTHEOFFBEAT@GMAIL.COM

DATE: MAR 11 AT 2:09 PM

SUBJECT: RE: BIG APPLE SHENANIGANS

Agreed.

Also interesting: the fact that we're emailing when we're literally sitting on a porch swing together. Shall we find another way to occupy those hands?

FROM: HOURTOHOUR.NOTETONOTE@GMAIL.COM

TO: BLUEGREEN118@GMAIL.COM

DATE: MAR 24 AT 6:12 PM

SUBJECT: OOF

Just got back to my dorm, and I guess you're somewhere in New Jersey by now. So how does this go again? Right, here's the part where I stare at my laptop screen trying to drudge up a shred of positivity. So . . . that was really good. We got sixteen days together, and obviously that's pretty extraordinary. Um.

I don't know, Bram. I'm just so tired of how bad it always feels to lose you. Remind me why we're doing this to ourselves again? My room feels so quiet without you, which just baffles me. Like, no one's out there giving you noise complaints, Bram Greenfeld. So maybe it's not actually quieter here—maybe it just feels quiet in my brain. I kind of want Kellan to come back and bother me. I texted him the all-clear as soon as we left for the train station, but I guess he's still in Grover's room. Because why the fuck wouldn't he be? If you lived in my building, I don't think I'd ever go outside.

I'm just exhausted from this. Like, is this even working for you?

FROM: BLUEGREEN118@GMAIL.COM

TO: HOURTOHOUR.NOTETONOTE@GMAIL.COM

DATE: MAR 24 AT 6:15 PM

SUBJECT: RE: OOF

Nope. It's not working.

Leah,

I know this email is three months late. More than three months. I don't even have a good excuse to give you. I just dropped the ball. And I guess I kind of dropped it on purpose. But your honesty here was such a huge fucking gift, and I just took it and never gave you any kind of honesty back. I'm really sorry. And I'm really grateful for your questions.

I'm going to try to answer every single one of them, okay?

I want to have sex with Bram for seventy years. I want to change diapers. I don't even want to think about taxes or health insurance, but if I HAVE to, Leah, then yeah. I want that with Bram. He's absolutely the person I want to spend my life with.

And I know this right now.

Though, I don't think I want it to *happen* right now.

But it's not like I *don't* want it to happen. And if he asked me tomorrow? I'd say yes. I wouldn't hesitate for a second. Okay, maybe *tomorrow* I'd hesitate (my inner goddess trusts NO ONE on April Fool's Day anymore. Nope).

Leah, I don't have a clue why I told Luke it was a marriage proposal. And I don't remember how it felt when I said it. Saying it out loud wasn't some kind of revelation for me. It already felt out loud. It's always felt out loud.

I hope I'm making sense (probably not). But I just want you to know how much your email helped me do this thing I need to do (something scary and exciting and extremely inevitable).

You're a fucking gem, Leah Burke, you know that?

Love,
Simon

Dear Blue,

I have to tell you something. And I'm so nervous about it, which is why I'm doing this in an email. I don't want to put you on the spot or forget to say stuff, and I really don't want to make anything weird. Which is probably a lost cause, but I'll give it a shot. COMMENCING: OPERATION SIMON SPIER DON'T BE WEIRD. (Welp. Going great already, I see.)

So I did a thing. And I guess I've been working on it for a couple of months now. But I've been really unsure if it's the right thing, or if YOU would think it's the right thing. And it might not even work out in the end. It's pretty much out of my hands now.

Bram, I applied to transfer next year. To NYU. I'm really sorry I didn't tell you sooner. But I wasn't sure I was going to go through with it. And B, I didn't want you to feel bad or guilty, or like you should be looking into transferring here. So yeah. I just wanted to do it and put it out into the universe, and we'll see what happens. It looks like I'll find out in May.

But, okay, the first thing you should know is this: If I get in, we're making this decision together. I don't want to crowd you (I know it's New York, lol, but you know what I mean). I know it would be a big change for us, and maybe it's too much. I don't know. I'm just saying, nothing's set in stone yet.

And I also want you to know that I don't see this as a sacrifice. Because I wouldn't be giving anything up. The only year that's been even partially written is this one. Everything else is wide open. It's the weirdest thing, B, because now I don't even know where I'll graduate. But this is my freshman year, you know? And I think it was supposed to be here. My tiny little Philadelphia nerd school with my weirdo roommate who, god help us, will probably be in our wedding one day. Bram, you wouldn't believe how much I fell in love with this place the minute I knew I wanted to transfer. I know that sounds completely absurd, but it all just feels so precious right now. Like it's not a place that's keeping us apart. It's just a place. And it's a place I get to keep, no matter what. It's in my nesting doll now.

And maybe NYU will be too. It was really fun to go back there. I took all these selfies in front of the arch, just to try and see what NYU Simon would look like (he looks a lot like regular Simon with a giant zit, if you were wondering). It's so different from Haverford. Like, it's different in every single way, to the point where I can't even imagine what living there would feel like. Maybe I'd just spend three years missing Haverford.

But at least I wouldn't have to miss you.

So now you know. And, Bram, you don't have to respond anytime soon. Just think about it, and sit with the idea, and then whenever you're ready, we can talk about it. And I promise, B, I promise you can tell me if you feel weird about it. We can pretend I never even applied. We don't have to mention it ever again, okay? I know how to be in love with you from Philly. Easy peasy. I could do it in my sleep.

Love,
Jacques

FROM: BLUEGREEN118@GMAIL.COM
TO: HOURTOHOUR.NOTETONOTE@GMAIL.COM
DATE: MAR 31 AT 11:20 PM
SUBJECT: RE: I MUST REALLY LIKE YOU.

Pressing pause. Saving the game. Calling you now.

Love,
Bram

ACKNOWLEDGMENTS

I've spent five years swearing I'd never write this story, and here we are. All I can say is this: Maybe it's a good thing, the way we never stop surprising ourselves.

This project has been pure joyful chaos, and I'm so grateful to the MVPs who dove in with me headfirst:

Donna Bray, Holly Root, Mary Pender-Coplan, Anthea Townsend, Ebony LaDelle, Sabrina Abballe, Jacquelynn Burke, Tiara Kittrell, Shona McCarthy, Mark Rifkin, Alison Donalty, Jenna Stempel-Lobell, Chris Bilheimer, and my teams at Balzer + Bray/HarperCollins, Root Literary, UTA, and Penguin UK. I'm in such awe. You made publishing miracles happen.

Isaac Klausner, Temple Hill, and everyone involved in *Love, Simon* and *Love, Victor*—especially Isaac Aptaker and Elizabeth Berger, who changed the course of Simon's life in a single email.

Caroline Goldstein and Emily Townsend, for the Haver-wisdom.

Aisha Saeed and Olivia Horrox, who watched me stare at my Word document on many trains and planes.

Adam Silvera, Nic Stone, Angie Thomas, and Mackenzi Lee, who let me borrow their universes.

Jasmine Warga, David Arnold, Dahlia Adler, Jenn Dugan, Matthew Eppard, Katy-Lynn Cook, and everyone else who kept my panic at bay during the deadline-homeschool two-punch.

Jaime Hensel, Sarah Beth Brown, and Amy Austin, who proved that Creekwood kids never lose touch.

My family, especially Brian, Owen, and Henry (funny how the love letters write themselves when it comes to you guys).

The Trevor Project, for giving my readers a shore worth swimming to.

And the readers who, after five years of no, still showed up for my yes.

**TURN THE PAGE FOR
A SNEAK PEEK AT**

New York Times Bestselling Authors
**BECKY ALBERTALLI
& ADAM SILVERA**

**HERE'S
TO
US**

The sequel to **WHAT IF IT'S US**

FROM

CHAPTER TWO

ARTHUR

Friday, May 15th

"What if you just . . . don't go."

"To the car?"

"To New York."

I stare at him, and he stares back through his glasses, his eyes plainly serious.

"Mikey." I shake my head. "I have a job—"

"You had one in Boston too," he says softly.

My stomach twists. "I should have told you sooner. Mikey, I'm so—"

"Stop. You don't have to apologize again." He shakes his head, cheeks flushed. "I'm just not ready for tomorrow."

"Me either." I sink onto the bed beside him.

"I wish you were still coming to Boston."

The song switches—"Heart of Stone." I take Mikey's hand, lacing my fingers through his. "Well, luckily it's just two months."

"Ten weeks."

"Fine, ten weeks. But it'll go by so fast, I promise. We won't even have time to miss each other."

He smiles sadly. "I kind of miss you already."

I look up at him, so startled I lose my breath for a second. *I kind of miss you already.*

I mean, I know Mikey's into me. I've never doubted that. But he's not usually quite so direct about it.

"Me too. But at least I get you back in two weeks." I nudge him sideways. "And I'm taking you to every single one of my favorite places. Central Park, Times Square, Levain Bakery, you name it."

Mikey's brow furrows.

I narrow my eyes. "What?"

"I didn't say anything."

"You made an eyebrow face."

Mikey disentangles our hands. "It's just." He pauses, rubbing the back of his neck. "Did you go to those places with Ben?"

"Oh. Well, yeah." I feel suddenly flustered. "But that was two years ago. Ben and I haven't even talked in ages. Since February."

Mikey shrugs like he doesn't quite believe me.

But it's true. It's been months since Ben and I have talked or even texted. I even tried FaceTiming him on his birthday in April, but he didn't pick up. And he definitely didn't call back.

Mikey's looking at me now with his basset hound eyes. "Are you going to see him?"

"You mean Ben?"

"You'll be in the same city."

"Mikey, seriously. I haven't talked to him since February. He doesn't even know I'm coming."

"I think he knows."

There's something about the way Mikey says it.

"What do you mean?"

The song switches again. "I Don't Need Your Love." I swear I can hear Mikey's heartbeat change tempo. He leans sideways, gropes around for my phone, and passes it to me. The Instagram notification pops up the moment I tap the screen.

@ben-jamin liked your photo.

It's the first time Ben's liked one of my photos in months.

My heart leaps into my throat. I've been trying not to let the Instagram thing bother me. It's normal for people to drift, right? Especially when it's your ex-boyfriend.

I just didn't think it would happen to *us*. To Ben and me. I kind of thought we were indestructible.

And in the beginning, we were.

I'll never forget that first week back home after leaving New York. Ben and I talked every single night until our phone batteries died. And for the rest of senior year, we never went more than a day without texting. I used to walk around the house on FaceTime so often, my parents started shouting, "Hi, Ben," whenever they saw my phone. Then sometimes Diego and Isabel would shout back, and the four of them would be off and running with some side conversation. Ben and I complained about it constantly, but I think we both secretly loved that our parents were lowkey obsessed with each other.

I mean, I liked to think Ben and I were lowkey obsessed with each other too.

And I thought college would be the same. Or better. Definitely better, because at least I wouldn't have to deal with my mom's knowing looks every time I stepped out of my bedroom. For the record, that's a barrel of laughs: trying not to be in love with your ex-boyfriend when he rants adorably about story structure over FaceTime *and* having your parents see right through every single denial. All the boyfriend-related parental scrutiny without the actual boyfriend.

So. Privacy was good. And Wesleyan's proximity to New York was even better. Just over three hours by train—two if I left my car at Bubbe's house and took the train from New Haven. Not that I expected our relationship to pick right up where we left it— not necessarily. But Ben seemed really happy I was moving closer. He brought it up constantly for months.

But once I was actually *in* Connecticut, things got weird really fast.

We still talked all the time, and Ben was always saying he missed me. Or I'd wake up to rambling "remember when" texts. But when I mentioned train schedules, he'd change the subject so fast it made my head spin.

Once, he sent me a screenshot of my own Instagram selfie, followed by a single heart eye emoji. Which led to two hours on FaceTime with Ethan and Jessie, trying to pinpoint the most casual-yet-effective way to say *um I think you're joke-flirting, but in case you're also real-flirting, might I remind you that I have a single dorm room.*

It was bewildering and infuriating and I was a Ben-addled mess all over again. I thought about blocking his number. I thought about showing up on his doorstep. I was surrounded by cute boys with loud opinions who liked kissing, so I tried that. But I always ended up alone in my fancy single dorm room, poring over Ben's texts.

Until Mikey.

@ben-jamin liked your photo.

I can't stop staring at the notification. Of course, it doesn't say which photo he liked. Could have been my packing day post, sure. But it could have also been the Stacey Abrams quote graphic I reposted last night, or Sunday's throwback photo for Mother's Day, or anything, really. I want to click into the app so badly my fingers are twitching, but I can't do that in front of Mikey.

That little heart icon.

I wish I knew what it meant.